Dominant + Violent + Hot = An Alpha Male

Alpha + Omega Wolf-Shifters, Volume 0.5

Lori Laidlaw

Published by Lynda French, 2025.

This is a work of fiction. Similarities to real people, places, or events are entirely coincidental.

DOMINANT + VIOLENT + HOT = AN ALPHA MALE

First edition. July 7, 2025.

ISBN: 978-1998074532

Written by Lori Laidlaw.

Table of Contents

To those who can embrace and love their true nature.

Marseille

My very first glimpse of an ocean didn't disappoint. I know that the Mediterranean is actually a sea, but it's huge and the biggest body of water I've ever seen. I was excited to see the color, the waves, and the way the water pushes the horizon far off into the distance.

That sight met all my expectations, but as I drew closer to the city of Marseille my senses were overwhelmed by the oppressive stench. My inner wolf's sense of smell, the most powerful of its senses, was painfully offended.

It wasn't until years later, when I inhaled a fresh breeze off the Pacific Ocean on a West Coast beach, that I realized the repellent odor I'd known in France was caused by the detritus of man, not the water itself.

Ever present in the port of Marseille is the iodine saltiness of seaweed and shellfish shriveling in the sun, caught on the sides of dinghies, and trapped in thick-hemped nets. Along with the debris of rotting fish carcasses, guts, and heads, the smell rises from the silvery scales stuck on every surface. Each berth in the marina has its own iridescent swirl of oily spillage from the marine diesel of the boats. It all reeks.

The rough part of town, where l live and work, is overhung by a miasma of sea stink. It clings to the clothes and bodies of the men who scrape out a living on the boats. It's embedded in the wooden walls of the homes, businesses, and bars. I'm already miserable, cranky, and irritated by my exile so the disgusting stench just makes everything worse.

When I catch a reflection of my face I'm wearing a permanent scowl with my upper lip lifted in a snarl. I can see that despite my forbidding expression the handsomeness of my face isn't diminished. But only very desperate or very drunk women ever make advances to me, the rest are sensibly repelled.

I'm almost nineteen years old and ready to fuck anyone willing and at times even those who aren't.

The gang who took me on are known colloquially as *Les Requins*, meaning *The Sharks* but I never did find out their full name. Fleeing from that false accusation in Hungary I traveled west across Europe working day laborer and cash jobs until joining this criminal outfit. I've had months and months of this life doing the jobs I'm assigned, getting paid, getting laid, and getting drunk.

My assignments are basically me spending hours doing nothing. Just standing around watching and waiting. The boredom, the dull and dreary routine, is offset by the stability of a steady income but shit... I'm too young to waste my life like this. Technically I'm guarding the product and the sellers, but nothing ever happens. Well, there was that incident last week when some scumbag attacked one of our distributors.

These women are reliable workers but they're no good at defending themselves. Desperate junkies driven by their frenzied cravings are a constant threat, plus the greedy opportunists looking for easy marks to rob.

That's what happened when Rose, an older woman, got knocked down and ripped off by a mugger. He ran, but I was on him in moments and got both the money and drugs back. Plus a great deal of satisfaction laying down a beating on him. That asshole will have plenty of time to regret messing with a Les Requins seller while he waits for his broken fingers, wrist, arm, and shoulder to heal.

I took Rose to a clinic to get fixed up and used some of the proceeds to pay the bill. That seemed only fair to me but her friends acted like I was some kind of hero. I got laid three nights in a row in appreciation.

It was great to fuck friendly girls without having to pay. I enjoyed being able to play and relax. They taught me plenty about giving women pleasure. We kissed, too.

I've kept my dual nature secret and that secret has prevented me from forming friendships. I guess I'm the stereotype of an unhappy, solitary teenager resigned to a lonely life.

Early one evening, returning from a job with two workmates, I'm summoned to meet Arnaud, the kingpin. The other youths look at me sideways and won't meet my eye. My stomach churns with worry but despite the turmoil inside I keep my face impassive when I'm brought before the powerful man. Nothing in the boss's expression gives a clue as to whether this meeting is good news or bad.

"Antal Szémosa, a wanted man on the run. A young man who has worked his way up from street runner to foot soldier simply through his exceptional brute strength."

Uncertain if a reply is expected I dip my chin in acknowledgement but stay silent. I'm waiting and wary since my incredible strength comes from my wolf.

The kingpin grins widely and turning to his second-in-command says: "Marcel, we were right. This one has brains and discretion to go along with his strong body."

Giving me his attention once again the kingpin explains: "We've been watching you for this past year and have a job for you. You will enter into intense training with my enforcer Severu the Sicilian. When he determines you're ready – so long as that's within ten days," he adds to laughter from those gathered, "you will accompany my eldest son to America.

The violence of the drug wars threaten Benet's life and my heir still has much to learn before he takes over. You will be his bodyguard and protector while he develops his negotiating skills, builds a network of contacts, and gets his hands dirty and bloody. That is my plan for you, so what do you say Antal Szemosa?"

"I am deeply honored, Sir."

Clapping his hands jovially the kingpin stands and approaching me reaches out to clasp my upper arms. My biceps are well-developed but I hold still and don't flex. This is supposed to be a friendly gesture but the ice-cold glare from Arnaud's eyes gives me a chilling warning. "You're right, it is an honor. And it's a sworn duty to perform to death."

Lifting my chin and meeting the commanding man's eyes I aver: "I swear it." And I mean it, too.

Severu steps forward. He's a mountain of a man with a shiny bald head, black eyes, and a thin-lipped mouth with gold-capped teeth. Severu's a chain-smoker who carries the smell of tobacco around in his car, on his clothes, and on his person. Nicotine-stained fingers, wrinkles around his eyes as he squints through the smoke from the ever-present cigarette, and a constant throat-clearing cough. His deep voice has a gravelly rasp.

I never do learn if Severu is the man's first name or his last. I don't know if he's married or has a family. I don't even know where he lives. Looking me up and down with a sneer Severu makes it clear that ten days isn't long enough to fully train an apprentice.

Shaking his head he explains: "I'll do what I can, but it will be all work. There will be no conversation between us, just lessons and instruction. We aren't friends, kid."

Again I nod instead of speaking thinking *at least it'll be a change, and with the bright prospect of ending up in America!*

Lessons in Brutality

Arriving at the address Severu texted me I'm surprised that the torture training area is inside a gym. I can see both standing and hanging punching bags, a roped-off boxing ring, and several sizes of dumbbells. The unmistakable stink of stale male sweat permeates the air, but it's a natural smell and doesn't offend me.

The chains hanging from the ceiling and embedded in the concrete floor, right beside an inlaid drain, reveal the true purpose of this venue. Especially when combined with the coppery tang of spilled blood. A variety of impact and cutting tools – everything from whips to bone-saws – hang inside a large metal cabinet on wheels.

One of the men noisily pulls a retractable wall along a track catching my attention. This opens up the space to include a room furnished like an operating theater except the bed has restraints attached, two small barred cells, and a tank for liquids. *For waterboarding? or is it filled with acid for dissolving bones and bodies?* I wonder, but I don't dare ask.

One of the doors along the far wall opens and Severu steps through. He's shirtless showing that every inch of his well-muscled chest is decorated with tattoos. His usual air of menace is intensified. This is clearly Severu's domain.

Suddenly I'm apprehensive, my senses on alert, despite being fifteen to twenty years younger than my mentor. My core self, the wolf within, recognizes that Severu is the apex predator in this aggressive, masculine milieu.

"You're late, boy."

"I'm not–" I begin but Severu just jerks his head towards the ring.

Jumping up I yank off my pullover, tossing it in a corner. My faded jeans won't hinder me, they're baggy enough to conceal weapons and easy to move in. Severu folds his powerful arms across his chest, settling back to watch.

Two men wearing boxing trunks join me in the ring. They swagger and smirk with confidence. They're both obviously unarmed but since the odds are stacked against me I'm prepared to fight dirty.

Blue Shorts circles behind and with a sudden lunge grabs me at the hips trying to wrestle me down to the ground. I'm expecting this move and using his body for leverage I swing my legs up delivering a hard kick to Black Short's chest. That man staggers back a couple of steps while I roll myself forward propelling Blue Shorts over my shoulders to crash down onto his partner.

Black Shorts recovers first wildly zooming into me so I grab the man's forearm and deftly bow and turn, somersaulting him to the floor. My opponents aren't so cocky now.

Taking each other's measure the fighting escalates until all three of us begin to flag. I lose my balance while ducking a haphazardly thrown punch and fall to my knees. Black Shorts seizes the opportunity to leap on top of me but I fell him with a cosh.

Laughing, Severu barks out: "No knife, boy?"

That startles Blue Shorts into whipping his head around. Taking advantage of my foe's distraction I lurch up and clip the back of Blue Shorts neck dropping him beside the first man. I'm a no-holds-barred street fighter.

I'm the victor but still bruises bloom and blood drips from me. Severu doesn't offer congratulations, instead, he nimbly leaps into the ring and rolling his shoulders gives a shark-like grin. With the warning that *if you pull a weapon on me I'll take it and use it against you* the two of us commence fighting. The fallen men recover enough to reel out of the way of our battle.

I find my second wind but the immovable weight of the bigger man's sheer bulk blocks me. Drawing deep inside my reserves I summon my wolf's strength but now I have to struggle against shifting. My wolf urges me to free him so he can bite and ravage our enemy's throat. Instead I take hold of Severu's neck and squeeze with my powerful hands.

Severu knows better than to try to pry an attacker's fingers loose. Instead he punches up into my elbows to break the strangling hold. The pain shooting through my forearms makes me grunt even as I tighten my grip.

I don't know who can hold on the longest but luckily for me Severu taps out so I immediately release him. My wolf's chagrin comes out in a snarl. The feral beast is disappointed. He wanted to hold on just a few seconds longer to establish dominance.

Rubbing his throat Severu nods in approval. His voice is even raspier when he declares: "You can fight, kid. Hard, fast, and dirty."

I'm panting for breath myself. Shrugging, I state: "I have two brothers, both older than me," in explanation.

"And are your brothers pretty boys like you?"

That surprises a laugh out of me. "They're not as handsome but yeah, the girls don't complain. Well actually they do complain about my oldest brother because he gets rough with them."

"Hmm, so you fight over these girls?"

"Sure, yeah. But we fight all the time, over anything and everything."

Nodding in understanding Severu continues: "As the youngest you had to learn how to fight the hardest, and as the prettiest they'd want to damage your face for sure."

Again I grin at him saying: "But as you can see they didn't succeed."

Severu snorts but his lip twitches, his version of smiling. He jumps down and gestures for me to follow. When I reach for my vee-neck Severu tells me to leave it off.

He leads the way to the torture area and indicates a chair with cuffs for ankles and wrists already attached. I cast a leery eye over the apparatus but can't spot any electronics. Gingerly, I sit down but there are no spikes or other sharp objects in the seat. My mentor's eyes are alight with amusement and that's a scary sight.

"Over the next hour or so I'm going to hurt you, Antal. I'm not going to maim you. No one respects an enforcer who is missing fingers, an eye, or a limb. But I will let you, well truth is I'll *make* you, sample pain. It's important to know how it feels from your victim's perspective."

Severu is a sadist who enjoys the suffering he inflicts with this training. His gaze is burning, excited by bloodlust. He doesn't secure me to the chair but I know I've been challenged and this is a test.

"No one can withstand interrogation indefinitely, but the mind can be taught to detach. It doesn't save the body from pain, but it lessens your discomfort. That's something you're gonna have to learn on your own time. My job is to show you how to incur the most damage to your victims.

As an enforcer some of your time will be spent interrogating, but you'll also be called on to punish. Quick clean deaths are reserved for heroes, not traitors, backstabbers, or thieves. Anyone who steals from your gang has betrayed each and every member. If your leader calls for their death it must follow a painful session that serves as a lesson, a deterrent to warn off anyone else with those same ideas."

Producing a scalpel Severu holds the instrument up for me to see it clearly. Neither of us speak and after a long moment Severu lightly traces a line down my breastbone. Keeping his hand within my line of sight Severu carefully marks my chest with bloody stripes. The cuts are shallow and they sting, but the pain is certainly bearable.

That is until Severu reaches down for a package standing upright on the ground. It's already open so he just has to scoop his hand inside. He shows me his palm is full salt. I feel my eyes widen and am sure my pupils dilate when I see what he's got. He rubs the salt into my sliced skin and I hiss a deep inhale. The coarse salt absorbs my blood and clings to the cuts in pink clumps. The pain never eases, each moment of contact is excruciating. I have to fight the urge to scrub it all off.

"Now imagine those same cuts, filled with salt, on your cock and balls. Or on your eyelids, bleeding through to your eyes and draining back into your skull. Simple and effective. With very little mess to clean up, and believe me boy, that's an important consideration. Especially when your time is limited or your location is compromised."

He tosses me a wet rag and I clean the bloody salt away as quickly as I can. It leaves me with a throbbing ache. I don't want to even imagine my balls feeling this kind of torment. Thankfully I passed this morning's tests.

Each day we meet early in the morning when I report to Severu for the training sessions. Severu demonstrates his technique on me, although he usually doesn't follow through completely, thank fuck.

We break up our lessons with extreme workouts and sparring in the ring. At mid-afternoon I go home to eat and sleep for a couple of hours before returning for work at night. Sometimes Severu will have a miscreant in the gym to victimize, but more often we go out *for fieldwork* as he puts it.

At some point every night we meet up with the kingpin, usually at the bar the gang owns, and Benet is always in attendance with his father. I'm certain me and him will work well together.

Benet is friendly without being overly familiar, confident without arrogance. I respect him for his position as the heir, and for his straightforward open nature. I'm happily looking forward to my future, working with this young boss in America.

Our ten days of scheduled training gets cut short after just six days despite Severu's complaints. Credible threats have been made against Benet, and Marcel warns the kingpin that the situation is dire. The gang wars have escalated to the point where Arnaud insists that ready or not the move has to happen now.

Severu spits on the floor to show his displeasure but states: "I need the boy for tonight."

Arnaud nods his permission and announces: "Okay so the plane will leave in about eighteen hours. Everybody go home and pack two suitcases, box up your stuff for storage, visit your bank, fuck your girlfriend, give notice to your landlord, whatever you need to do get it done and meet back here by 7:00 tomorrow night. The plan is to load up the plane and get clearance from Air Traffic Control so you can be in the air by 9:00 pm. What time will they land, Marcel?"

"If I've figured out the time change thing right it will be about midnight New York time, and that's 6:00 in the morning for us. If you wear a watch you'll have to set it backwards. By time everybody deplanes and travels to the hotel you'll be ready to sleep for a few hours then wake up like everybody else in New York City."

There's confusion on some faces but I think I've got it figured out. The half-dozen men in this crew are young and ready for adventure.

Severu tells me: "We'll be up late tonight so go get some sleep now. Your errands can wait until tomorrow, there can't be all that much for you to do. I'll text you when and where to meet in a few hours."

Stay Away from Bad Men

I jerk up in bed, my body slick with sweat and my heart racing. *It's only a dream, only a dream* I keep repeating to myself. I'm gasping for air, desperate to fill my lungs.

Since I've always had an unusually low heart rate, at least according to our family doctor, this fearful panic sends sharp pains stabbing into my chest. As the terror of the nightmare slowly fades so does the unaccustomed pulsing of my blood. It actually hurts when it pounds that hard.

I can recall enough of the dream to know it's that recurring one where I viciously attack Beáta. In real life I never once harmed her, but that all changes when I'm asleep. In dreamland I savagely thrill at the bloody violence I'm inflicting on her young body. I'm acting out punishment and revenge, justice and retribution.

My phone is lit up so it must have been the *ding* of an incoming message that woke me. Thank fuck, I think, shivering at the fading memory of the nightmare.

The text is an address with Severu demanding that I *come now.*

The street is familiar and close by. It's home to a couple of low dives, a massage parlor, and some condemned warehouses. I'd like to wash my dream-sweat off first but there's never any hot water at this time of day.

I consider grabbing a quick cold shower but shake my head realizing being on time for Severu is more of a priority then me smelling clean. Especially where I'm headed. If I'm stinking I'll blend in even better at this location.

Arming myself with my usual weapons of a knife, brass knuckles, and my gun, I leave my building soundlessly.

The derelict building I arrive at is hosting a rave. Two DJs work the spinning turntables and colored lights flash in sync with the amplified techno music. A young crowd dances packed tightly together inside this rickety fire trap.

Through a cloud of cigarette and marijuana smoke I spy Severu with some men from the *Requins* crew in the far corner. They're hovering around one of the makeshift bars which are really just wooden tubs filled with bottled beer on ice.

The server is a young, heavyset girl with a pretty face and fluorescent red hair pulled into two buns on each side of her head. I think she looks like something out of a sci-fi space movie.

Look at those tits, I think, *they're incredibly fucking huge.*

She's seated, but from what I can see her hips are generously-sized and her thighs spread in smooth mounds. Clothes that are too tight and too short show that she's fat, but proportionate. Her skin glows an unblemished, creamy white. A body built to warm the bed and provide comfort to any man.

Severu is casually leaning against a wall, arms crossed, body relaxed as he watches the interplay between his men and the girl.

High-pitched giggles show that she's excited by, but also apprehensive of, their heated attention. They press in too close and although no one's hands have strayed yet it's obviously only a matter of moments before the groping will begin and then the fighting will start.

Just as tensions peak Severu pushes forward and the men resentfully step back to make room for him.

The *Requin* enforcer is such a large man he makes the chunky girl look small as he easily lifts her off the chair and seating himself plops her down in his lap.

Her giggles are a stutter and she hiccups a few times, grinning widely. The effect her rapid breathing has on her half-exposed tits has the men mesmerized with their eyes glued to the quivering mass of flesh. When Severu palms the underside of each breast to lift and then push them together there's a collective sigh.

The girl tries to pull his hands away but he draws her back against his massive chest and nuzzles along the side of her neck.

He rumbles in her ear: "You like teasing these boys with your luscious tits, don't you little girl?" and she arches her back, thrusting her chest out. Severu is now massaging each breast in a circular motion and the thin cloth can't hide how her hard nipples poke out.

The neckline of her blouse is elasticized and Severu nudges it down off her shoulders with his mouth. He frees up a hand to pluck the front open and tilting her head to one side he leans over to take a long look at her naked flesh.

"They all want to know what color your nipples are, and how big, and how hard," he murmurs but loud enough for everyone to hear.

Looking up he informs the men that *they're sweet little cherries ripe for licking and nipping and sucking.* Then he gnashes his teeth and growls into her neck while she squeals with a heady mix of pleasure and fear.

The girl's mind is whirling with thoughts and ideas. She's whispering, but with my wolf's acute hearing her words are perfectly clear to me.

My body is actually tingling, I'm hot and cold with shivery sensations. This is all kinds of wrong but I've never felt so alive. Still... I'm kinda scared about how far things will go. I mean, I'm pretty sure I've already lost control of the situation, but I can still control myself? Can't I?

"The boys are going to leave us now but you owe them something for all your teasing. Pull down your blouse and shake those tits, flash them with a nice show before they go," Severu commands.

The girl protests but he simply tightens his hold on her and orders: "Obey me, little one."

One of the men chants *show us show us* and others join in and start clapping. The girl bites her bottom lip seductively, reveling in the attention, and with a gasp quickly pulls her top down over her arms to her elbows.

Her exhibitionism makes her feel daring. Especially when she shakes her shoulders and the lovely round globes shimmy to the appreciative groans of all the males. Her swollen nipples jut forward from large dusky areolae.

Performing for an audience has her squirming with excitement and Severu encourages her by sliding her soft, fleshy bum back and forth over his crotch.

With a jerk of his head he sends the men away but calls: "Antal, you stay. We're going to have another training session."

Taking hold of the girl's wrists he pulls her arms behind her back and her bare breasts wobble. Gesturing for me to kneel in front and enjoy I'm quick to obey, happily thrusting my face into that pillowy softness.

Squeezing and kneading her flesh I suck on first one nipple then the other and back again. All the while Severu is quietly talking to the girl in his deep, gravelly voice.

"You love being the center of attention, don't you? And you love how the men all stare and drool over your big tits and you love the power that gives you."

I watch the girl confusedly answer *yes* and *no* before she becomes totally distracted by the pleasure of my touch and the deep voice of this powerful dominant man.

Severu teases her with sexy innuendo, insults, and praise.

"You're my horny little slutty tease, aren't you?" he murmurs in her ear before licking it then blowing out his breath until shivers run down her neck goosebumping all her flesh. "I bet you're still a virgin, eh? Always ready to clamp your thighs shut tight once you've got the boys all excited, hmm?"

The girl isn't paying attention, she's staring at me awestruck. She has no idea I can hear her murmuring.

Such a gorgeous face. He's about my age, maybe a year or two younger or older. He's so handsome, and he has such a penetrating stare with his dark eyes. It's like he's looking right into the very heart of me. His hair is light brown and long enough to run my fingers through if only my hands were free... but the glimpse of chest I see through his unbuttoned shirt shows fine black hairs. He is full of contrasts. I've never been with such a handsome man.

"What a pretty girl you are, and being so good for Antal, letting him touch your tits as much as he wants. Look how he plays with you, you're utterly helpless with his hands all over you, his eyes getting their fill. Do you want me to play with your body, too? I can make you feel so good."

"Oh, oh," she cries softly as his lips send another wave of shivers up and down her neck. With my keen sight I can see the tiny hairs lift and I know she's primed.

"You're just a naughty little thing, aren't you? You're such a bad girl for teasing the boys like that. You like knowing how much they want to see your tits, touch them, taste them. You flaunt them like a little cocktease. You should be punished for that behavior. Wanton little slut."

"I'm not!" she exclaims but then a low moan escapes her and she forgets her indignation. She's given up trying to free her hands and instead accepts my ministrations to her exposed breasts with enjoyment. I'm busy studying and exploring them, squeezing, teasing, and toying with her while listening to her softly grumble.

My nipples ache, they feel like they're gonna burst, omigod he knows! he knows exactly what I'm feeling because he's grazing them with his teeth and gently biting down. Ungh, the pressure is too much! I feel them swelling, I want him to take as much in his mouth as he can and suck hard, I want him to squeeze hard!

"Boys don't know what to do with a sexy little baby like you. You don't need boys, you need a man. A firm-handed man, heavy-handed man who will put you in your place and keep you there. A man you will want to submit to and please. Do you want to please me, baby girl?"

She shakes her head *no* but her thighs have fallen open and she's unwittingly tilted her pelvis up.

He sees right through me! His lips kissing me, his hot mouth lightly sucking my neck, but fuck it's his words that are driving me crazy. He's a real grown-up man. I want to beg him to take charge of me. Take away all my decisions and let me revel in the pure pleasure his voice promises.

I don't think Severu can hear half of what she's saying but I'm entertained by every one of her unguarded thoughts.

"No? Well if you don't want to please me then I guess you need to be punished, hmmm?" Severu cups her pussy with the palm of his hand

and rubs hard. The girl squirms and utters little gasping cries of *please* and *it's too much* then in contradiction, *more, I need more!*

"Oh yes you need some discipline, babygirl. Do you want a spanking? Do you want Daddy to put you across his knee?"

I'm following her whispered commands to keep pinching her nipples, squeezing her breasts, and kissing them all over. The soft pleading sounds the girl makes have me rock hard. Severu keeps tormenting her clit while still holding her hands behind her back. The strong scent of her arousal is a turn on for all three of us.

Severu continues his rumbled promises and threats. "Oh yeah, you want to be properly punished with a sound spanking on your bare bottom." I don't understand all the words but I can *get by* in half-a-dozen languages so I hear the alliteration and the cadence of his speech. And I can see the way the girl writhes in arousal.

Severu motions to me to sit back while he upends the girl over his knee. Her short skirt is easily pushed up and her fat derriere is naked except for the floss of a thong. Severu massages her rump, squeezing handfuls of goosebumped skin. Her bare flesh quivers in anticipation.

He begins spanking the girl, each smack resounding loudly as he moves his hand from one cheek to the next. Over and across, up and down, again and again. She's kicking her feet and squirming but her *oohs* and *ahhs* aren't from pain. Her scent strengthens and, impossibly, my cock gets harder.

"This is what you've been wanting, you wicked little girl. Acting up and being bratty, being a cocktease, flaunting your tits. You're just begging to be taken in hand and thoroughly spanked. Bad girl, naughty girl."

The girl's behind soon shows a tinge of light pink. She's getting a foreplay spanking, not hard, just enough of a sting to make her squeak *ooh! ooh!* and it's fucking hot.

Once again her thighs slip open revealing the damp patch on her thong. Severu pulls the thin material tightly between the glistening lips of her pussy. She widens her spread legs even more. While Severu keeps administering sharp, but light, strokes I finger her wet hole making the girl's hips buck rhythmically. I need to tamp down my urge to growl.

"You're enjoying your punishment, aren't you pet? Hmm? You bet you are. You like it when Daddy spanks his naughty girl's pretty bum while Antal diddles you." Severu's crooning has the girl moaning and wiggling. "Antal, undo your belt. Take it off."

I've been rubbing my cock through the thick denim of these jeans and now I'm eager to follow Severu's orders. I want to fuck this horny little slut whose bouncing pink cheeks and creamy thighs are so inviting.

Severu knows what I want but stops me saying: "No, no. We're not going to fuck her. We're going to give her a real punishment now. The spanking was just play but this belting will be torture. She's got to learn what a mistake it is to let bad men get her alone and naked.

Teach her a good lesson, boy. I'll hold her down while you whip all this abundant white flesh until it's raw red."

His words don't penetrate the lusty haze the girl is in and even I have to shake my head to clear it. My cock is disappointed, but the demon within me roars its bestial approval.

Winding back my arm to deliver a punishing blow I bring the leather down forcefully with a loud crack that's matched by the girl's shriek of pain. Her plump flesh rippled with the strike and now it quivers as an angry red stripe forms.

"Again! and harder this time," instructs Severu who stands to slide the girl off his lap and situate her face-down over the chair. He stays out of the reach of my swinging belt so it can't catch his legs. The girl's heavy breasts weigh her down, keeping her in place while Severu grips her by her upper arms. Her legs are kicking wildly as I give her a solid, painful thrashing.

Red welts stripe her whole ass and carry on right down to the back of her knees. I barely pause between swings and she's screaming and keening with the burning agony I'm unleashing. Her panic and pain drives me into a frenzied attack slashing back and forth, left and right, up and down – just like Severu did with his hand.

Luckily for her I'm holding the belt by the buckle-end or the metal would be tearing through her skin and leaving her bloody.

I admit to myself that although watching the girl wiggle her bare ass while being fingered and spanked turned me on, delivering this brutal beating makes me high. I want to bite down hard, I want to ravage every hole. I like this punishment shit because this is real pain, not a playful paddling. I'm hard and horny and the desire to hurt and harm is powerful.

Maybe I should have punished Beata. It was her lies that drove me from my home, sent me on the run, always hiding and fearful because of her false accusation. But no, someone said... it was my brother, my brother Gyuri who said Beata didn't remember anything about the attack so it couldn't have come from her. I guess people figured it must have been me because we'd broken up. She dumped me for my hated oldest brother, Kada. Ugh! Thinking of Kada makes me grit and grind my teeth.

"Beat her till she's burning and bruised. You need the training and she needs to learn this lesson."

I hear Severu's commands but feel myself detaching from any feeling. I've suppressed my arousal to concentrate on administering blow after blow, delivering the most effective punishment possible. The girl, the reason, none of that matters, I'm focused solely on this beating. Severu calls a halt and I stop, only now feeling the ache in my arm. Her skin is red and raw.

The girl's cries have dwindled down to hoarse groans as she gasps breaths through her snot and tears. She lies limp, silently weeping. Throughout this the music has blared, the lights have strobed, and across the room people have danced oblivious to the torturous session she's undergone in our secluded corner.

Severu pulls her to her feet and her knees cave. Taking hold of her upper arms he keeps her steady while peering into her red, teary face to ask: "Have you learned how dangerous it is to tempt and tease bad men, Charlotte?"

What? he knows her name? I jerk my chin up when Severu says this, and the girl is surprised as well.

"That's right, Charlotte. Tonight's lesson was planned. You've stopped listening to your aunt and uncle and been rude to them, claiming *they're not your parents and can't tell you what to do*. They don't have children of their own and have no idea how to handle you. They're worried because your parents left you in their care and they want to do their best. I offered to mete out a suitable discipline to get you back to behaving like a proper young lady. Have I succeeded in that?"

She nods her head vigorously, sending the dripping tears flying from her cheeks. Severu wipes them with his thumb saying: "I'm happy to repeat this lesson if necessary—"

"No! No, it won't be necessary," she stumbles through the words in her haste to say them. "Please! I promise! I promise I'll be good."

In a stern voice that even I find intimidating Severu states: "If you stop being a good girl and I have to visit you again your belting won't be confined to just your ass and thighs. I'll have these big tits whipped as well as your belly and pussy. That's what's in store for you if you stop obeying your guardians, Charlotte. Do you understand?"

Again, she frantically nods her head *yes!*

"Do you believe me?" he whispers.

Her face pales and her eyes grow round as she begs to assure him *I do, I won't, you'll never need...* Mentally I'm taking notes on how he speaks, his tone of voice, the measured words, and the girl's reaction.

"Fix your clothes," he says and watches impassively while she pulls her top up and her skirt down, wincing as the fabric rubs against her sore skin.

Oww, that hurts. My bum and the back of my legs hurt so much. I'm so embarrassed, I thought he... they... liked me and I wanted oh... I feel like such an idiot, they fooled me. And the young one looks so dreamy but he hurt me bad. I let them... ugh, I feel terrible, I'm so ashamed.

"I will escort you home and you will not return to this place or anywhere in this neighborhood. Not as an employee, not as a customer. Not ever. You've had your taste of the wild side and the memory will stay fresh every time you sit down for the next few days. Now you're going to behave yourself, right?"

"Yes, sir," the chastened girl affirms, struggling against the urge to start crying again.

Severu takes her by the arm, not roughly, and they head out of the venue. He catches my eye over the girl's head and winks, saying: "You go find yourself a whore who is willing to let you do what you have to and take what you need. You're flying out to a new place tomorrow so it might be awhile before you get another chance."

I know my face has darkened with lust from the way he smirks at me. I don't care. I'm off in search of a busty woman I can slap and bite while I fuck her hard.

Going Solo

Happily I find the woman I need almost immediately. It's not such a lucky occasion for her. I went straight to the Massage Parlor I passed on the way to the rave and explained what I want to the Madame.

A wicked smirk twists her thickly lipsticked mouth. "I have just the girl for you, handsome guy," she cackles evilly.

Calling out to someone in the room behind her she summons a burly man, the establishment's bouncer, and the two of them lead me up a flight of stairs to a hallway full of closed doors. The poor lighting can't hide the dust and dirt on a threadbare carpet. A musty smell of stale body sweat and semen hangs heavily in the air.

Reaching the last room the woman gestures for the man to unlock it saying: "Bruno, this fella is going to give Lola a good hiding before fucking every hole and I'm not even charging him the full rate."

Turning to me she adds: "I don't care if you mark her up, in fact I want you to mark her. Bruise her, maim her, the more damage the better. Bruno here is way too soft on these girls and this time Lola has gone too far."

I don't know what to say to that, but the man meets my eye and gives a nod.

The door swings open and I see a young dark-haired woman strung up by her wrists facing away from us. Looking over her shoulder she scowls in defiance.

One eye is blackened and blood streaks down from a cut on her swollen mouth. Her back, ass, and legs are crossed with the thin welts of a caning, some beading with blood. I assume this is Bruno's handiwork.

It's obvious from Lola's sneer that the cutting sting of the many, many strokes hasn't cowed her, but it sure looks like it should have. It must have hurt like a bitch.

"What did she do?" I ask, not caring if anyone bothers to answer. Severu has already driven home the lesson that *the why* doesn't matter so I'm not curious but I can sense that the Madame expects me to ask. Her answer is for Lola's benefit as much as mine.

"She's a mean bitch who bullies the other girls, extorting what little allowance they've earned, stealing or smashing any trifles they own, and brutalizing them in their beds.

See, I've always allowed the girls to cuddle and comfort each other, if they can enjoy an orgasm why not? sometimes they even think they're in love!

But this one has been damaging my merchandise by hurting some of the weaker girls. I have no room for such an angry, vicious cunt in my house. Punish her as a lesson to everyone else and then I'll throw her out."

Less than an hour ago I was beating the girl Charlotte on Severu's orders and had to suppress the excitement my body felt when she writhed and screamed. Now I can let the arousal flood back. I'm young and healthy, virile and easily stimulated. This isn't simply a naughty girl caught playing with fire no, this is a nasty wicked woman. Now it's her turn to experience what it's like to be a naked and helpless victim to someone's darkest desires. I intend to fully indulge myself, enjoying this tasty offer.

Stalking round Lola I study her from head to toe with a critical eye. She curses me and her ex-employer but I don't pay any attention. Turning her body so we're face-to-face I grip her throat with one hand while thrusting the fingers of the other into her dry pussy. Twisting and stretching my hand I reach her puckered anus with my thumb to plunge in fast and deep. She can't control how her pelvis twitches from the discomfort of my rough invasion.

Just in time I see Lola's cheeks working and before she can spit out the saliva she's gathered I release her neck and slam my open palm into her face, covering her mouth. She tries to bite but her teeth can't get a grip on the tight skin so she's forced to swallow back the drool that hasn't already leaked from her lips. With a quick snap I break her nose and blood gushes out. Ignoring her yells of pain I smear the blood over her cheeks and lips.

The proprietor nods in satisfaction and signaling to Bruno leaves the room. Before closing the door she warns me *if you end up killing the bitch you'll have to get rid of the body yourself.*

I acknowledge her with a nod, impatient to get back to the fun of breaking my new toy.

By giving Lola a taste of pain I've ratcheted up her anxiety levels. Now I use a tactic learned from Severu's first interrogation session: silence. Well, not quite silent, just voiceless. I make sure she can hear my footsteps as I pace back and forth behind her. I do that for a while and then I stop. Minutes later I clear my throat.

At first Lola tries to engage by swearing and tossing insults at me, then by making threats, then by offering rewards. After she resorts to her own silent treatment I wait and wait and wait – the only sound her ragged breathing – and then I crack a knuckle and chuckle when she flinches.

Over these past few days with Severu I decided I don't want to be an enforcer who pummels and punches, stomps and kicks, smashes and pounds, with all the finesse of a rabid dog attacking. I want to work

29

with clinical detachment, using the victim's own fear against them. Logical, effective, and goal-driven.

Finally I break the silence saying, almost conversationally, "From what I just heard from your boss you're a bully, Lola. You're also a thief, a destroyer, and sexual abuser," I pause while she argues then ignoring everything she's said, I continue: "I can't address each of your transgressions but I can certainly deal with the latter crime. I'm guessing you used a dildo to inflict pain. Hmmm, I'm looking around this room but I don't see one here."

Walking to the door and opening it I yell into the hallway: "I need a bottle of wine. A bottle with a nice long neck." I know my French is only passable so I'm not sure what will be delivered but am pleased when moments later Bruno comes in with a white Reisling in a Rhine bottle. It has a long slender neck and sloping shoulders. It's ideal.

"This is perfect," I declare, hefting the weight in my hand.

"Nobody likes this German shit," Bruno explains. He looks over at a trembling Lola curiously since no new marks have appeared on her body. Looking back at me his puzzled frown disappears and he says: "Oh you don't want the wine to drink..."

He trails off as a graphic image enters his mind. Bruno watches as I secure each of Lola's ankles to the cuffs on the bed legs. She's spread wide and the strain shows in her stretched torso.

"Nice," I murmur appreciatively, "but I want a better view of the action."

Reaching up I lift Lola's bound wrists from the ceiling hook and push her forward. She lands awkwardly on the bed, unable to block her fall, and I move around to position her to my liking. Piling the pillows under her belly lifts her pelvis in a way that exposes both her pussy and butt hole.

Standing back to admire the view I nudge Bruno who only grunts but I can see the man's erection growing in his pants.

My own arousal is in abeyance. I know I desperately need a hard, solid fucking but I've made up my mind that that won't be with Lola. I have no prurient interest in her, I only see her as my victim, she is nothing more than that.

Although I have no presentiment it will turn out that during my career of torture and interrogation I will never engage in sexual activity with my captives. I will abuse their genitals, they're such a sensitive area of the body. I'm content to satisfy myself with the hookers I hire for rough sex.

Picking up the bottle of wine I remark: "Oh good, it's capped. Much easier to work with." Unscrewing the cap I take a long swig straight from the bottle. Smacking my lips I comment: "Sweet, but I'm really not into wine." I hand the bottle to Bruno who takes a long drink but makes a face afterwards.

"This is the only lube you're going to get, Lola," I say as I pour the remains of the bottle over the girl's puckered back hole. Liquid runs down across her taint to her pussy lips.

She protests, her voice shrill and fearful, but I pay no attention. Pressing down on her lower back I position the top of the bottle at her anus and just before giving it a hard thrust whisper: "How does it feel to be on the receiving end, you vile bitch?"

Lola shrieks in pain, again and again as I keep up a steady pace driving the bottle inside her like a weapon. Plunging it in and out I block out the noise and concentrate on how her body reacts. Her legs are shaking, her back arches, her fisted hands are fighting the restraints. She tries to escape the invasion by squirming and writhing but she's only damaging her insides even more. Pulling the bottle out fully I now plunge it straight into her cunt. Streams of blood trickle down the cleft between Lola's butt cheeks. I'll bet this is exactly the same sight she saw when she was the abuser. I turn to point this out to Bruno but the older man has left and the door is closed.

I keep up a one-side conversation, replying to each of Lola's painful cries with a questioning comment:

Oomph, that one really hurt, didn't it?

I bet you used a really big dildo to rape your co-workers, didn't you?

So tell me, how many times did you hurt those girls like this?

Did it make you horny, Lola? 'cause this doesn't turn me on at all.

I continue the torment until Lola's breathing is raspy and her voice is too hoarse to shout any more. Blood, urine, and runny feces comes streaming out of her holes and I know her internal organs have ruptured. I expect she'll bleed out fairly quickly.

Bundling the bedding around her to absorb as much of the mess as possible I sit on the bed, up by her head, and watch her die. She doesn't look at me, her eyes are open but unfocused.

This is torture, this is vengeance and revenge, punishment and retribution, all rolled up in one. This is my calling... I'm lucky I've found my niche.

Even though her face is contorted in an agonized grimace I can see that she was a beautiful woman in life. *Well, beautiful on the outside,* I correct myself. *Her inside must have been rotten and twisted and black. Something like mine.*

While waiting to hear that final rattling breath I call Severu. It's very late now, but I know the man hardly sleeps. When he answers l come straight to the point: "I need a new lesson mentor, on how to dispose of a body."

Severu simply asks: "Where are you?"

An Unpleasant Truth

Severu arrives shortly after and the two of us carry Lola's body out of the Massage Parlor. People seeing what is obviously a corpse wrapped in a bloody bedsheet get the message and pass on the warning. Severu and I haul her several streets away before dumping her in an alley.

I get my first lesson in body disposal as Severu explains: "The unpleasant truth is that the bodies of prostitutes are the easiest since they don't even need to be hidden. Nobody gives a shit about these women, nobody is gonna look for them. From the moment they turn their first trick they're victims. Maybe even before, yeah, probably from when they were young and being hurt at home or kicked out onto the streets.

Female or male, child or legal age, doesn't matter, they are practically non-citizens – non-human even – as far as the authorities are concerned. They can be tossed in a dumpster, left in an alley, thrown in the water. Disposed of like fucking garbage."

We continue walking through the backstreets and stuff the bloody bedding down inside a dumpster, hiding it more than we did with the body. We're now far off from where we left her.

I suppose I should feel something like remorse but I don't regret a thing. Somebody needed to end Lola, and it turned out that somebody was me. I refuse to feel guilty for enjoying it.

We change direction again and enter another insalubrious part of town. Severu continues my lesson explaining:

"The best place to hide a body is at a construction site where it can be hidden forever once the concrete is poured. Same with fresh graves in cemeteries. I've got connections with people who notify me when something comes available. It costs, of course, but it's worth it.

If I have to I'll put a body in cold storage until a suitable spot comes up. It's always best to have a permanent solution.

Pigs are good too, but there aren't any pig farms in the city so it means moving the body. Traveling with a corpse is risky and there's always evidence left behind. Same with burial in the woods.

Dismembering, dissolving in acid, or feeding into a wood chipper all require a place with lots of room and privacy, plus there's heavy clean-up after. If you're really pressed for time drop the body off the side of a boat. It'll almost certainly come back, though."

His matter-of-fact delivery of these macabre instructions should be chilling but I hang on every word. Learning these lessons is vital to keeping me out of jail, or worse.

"Some times you need the body to be found so when that happens you want to leave it on a bike path or somewhere dog walkers go. One of those dog parks would be a great place. By time the cops show up the body would be all bitten and pissed on, but there's always somebody in those parks no matter what time of day or night. Someone's always out with their damn dog."

We've walked until arriving at a brothel. Severu says he's brought me here *to ease your itch and establish an alibi*.

The older man instructs the Madame to find me a girl *with big tits who can take a punch* but I interrupt him to tell her *it'll just be rough sex*.

He then heads down the hall to office of the whoremaster calling back to me: "I'll collect *Les Requins* protection fee and have a drink and a smoke with my old friend while waiting for you. No need to rush, we have lots to catch up on."

The criminal underbelly of Marseille is a small world so they'll pass the time sharing news of mutual acquaintances, and Severu will bring back the gossip to Arnaud and Marcel.

The Madame leads me up a narrow staircase and down a dimly-lit hallway, it's all so similar to the massage parlor from earlier. She unlocks a door and inside I see that it's sparsely furnished with a large bed and a small vanity with a sink and a mirror.

The girl lounging on the bed quickly stands, listening meekly to the Madame who instructs her in a voice that is harsh with sharp words. Her French is spoken too quickly for me to understand but the girl's bowed head and drooping shoulders indicate she is resigned to meeting whatever demands I make. I'm not going to punch her, but I will hurt her in other ways.

The Madame leaves and I listen to make sure she doesn't lock the door behind her, trapping me inside. Turning back to the girl I see a young woman, possibly a teenager still, wearing a torn pink nightie that exposes big breasts with dark nipples and a triangle of pubic hair centered between wide hips.

Her long dark hair and voluptuous figure remind me of Beáta. Beáta who betrayed me. The girl starts telling me her name – or at least her hooker name – but I stop her saying *you're Beáta to me.*

She nods agreeably, whatever I want, but what I want isn't her compliance but her destruction. Her tears, squeals, and screams. The hopeful way she's looking at me shows she's confusing a handsome face with a kind heart and that makes me mad. I'm gonna leave devastated and broken.

No doubt she thinks it will be easy to entertain a good-looking man who is close to her own age, despite the Madame forewarning her of my desires. She's been ordered to obey, and I'm going to lick every teardrop while ruining her.

I squeeze and twist the fleshy female parts until *this Beáta* is sobbing. My strong fingers clutch and pull at her skin while I grope with my hands and suck hard with my mouth. My teeth graze and then bite. After mauling her until the tears stream down her plump cheeks I yank her legs apart and covering her tender pussy with one hand I clench down tight. She whines at the pain.

Her indrawn breath is ragged as I brutally thrust my cock deep and hard into her cunt. The only sounds are her pitiful pleas and the slapping of skin on skin. My eyes roam with satisfaction over tender flesh red from my fingermarks and bruised by my teeth. I'm ready for my first release once her face is wet and each inhale is a gasp of pain.

Quickly flipping her onto her stomach I let loose a hot stream across her fat behind. Smacking and massaging my cum into her ass and over her thighs I collapse my full weight down on this hapless girl. Her skin is so soft and warm and damp with our sweat.

I love the powerful feeling I get from her smallness compared to my size, her submission to my dominance, her tears to my pleasure. I thread my fingers through her thick hair to clutch at her scalp. I know she's terrified I'll crush her skull or break her neck but instead I spew a mix of curses and endearments in my native tongue. I tell her she's my *csinos szuka [pretty whore]* and my *édes ringyo [sweet slut]*.

At nineteen I'm still a teenager and the stimulating sensation of my cock nestled in the cleft of her plump bottom quickly brings me to a second arousal. When I start moving my hips for friction *this Beáta* tells me I can have her small hole if I want, but we have to use lube.

38

My first thought is *I don't have to do anything* but I'm deeply interested, I've never had anal sex before.

What happened earlier with Lola wasn't sexual to me. I recall one time, years ago, when I stumbled into the wrong room and interrupted my friends Imre and Stefan in a compromising embrace. It didn't disgust me, in truth I was intrigued by the sight of a cock stroking in and out of a butt-hole.

Lifting myself off of *this-Beáta* I let her roll towards the vanity where she finds some greasy ointment. She also grabs a condom which she passes to me to unwrap. I'm puzzled, because we've already fucked without protection but then I realize this must be for my sake. *For safety? or for easy clean-up?* I'm too impatient to ask.

I roll it on and stroke my cock, squeezing along the length, while staring at her puckered hole. *This Beáta* awkwardly reaches behind and is dabbing lube around the area in a hit-or-miss fashion. I take over the job of oiling her butt-hole and then slip one finger half-an-inch in before I go deeper, twirling it around. I'm fascinated to feel heat and suction and I suspect I'm feeling muscle. She grunts a little but is relaxed while I explore.

This little hole looks way too small to fit me inside... but *this-Beáta* is pulling her butt-cheeks apart in invitation. With a growl I fit the head of my cock in place and start pressing into the hot tightness. The girl gives a few pained cries as I push my wide girth in until I've breached that tight inner ring. The sensation is like nothing I've ever felt before. It's fantastic and I love it.

I want her to wiggle and squirm so I command *play with yourself!* and she quickly snakes her hand between her legs to rub her clit. It's euphoria the moment she eases up enough to allow my full length inside.

So tight, so hot and now that I'm fully seated I relish how her round ass cushions me. Sliding in and out makes those cheeks first wobble then jiggle when I suddenly slam back into her.

I lift the girl up on to her knees so I can see my cock moving back and forth while stretching her small asshole. My balls bang against the wet lips of her pussy and when the moaning *this Beáta* cums my explosion within her choking confined space is actually painful. Pleasurably so.

I don't know if she really came or just pretended, but I don't care, I had a fantastic fuck and she doesn't have to fake anything for me.

I pull out and lean back on my knees so I can look at her red, sore hole. The only thing better would be if I saw my cum running out of it down to her cunt. I filled that hole the first time and when I reach inside to probe the wetness I accidentally discover a spongy area, her g-spot, with my curled finger. *This Beáta's* startled cry of pleasure is definitely the real thing and unexpectedly it makes me smile. I'm pleased with myself.

I give a final bite to her meaty shoulder before standing. The girl has been provided to me at no charge but I toss a handful of bills down beside her spent body. I'm grateful for the new thing she's shown me.

During my training with Severu I've acquired a reputation for violence and she probably feels lucky that her ordeal ended with no broken bones. I never permanently damage the women I fuck, but I might leave bleeding wounds.

In the future I will learn that I also became known as a generous man with an attraction to this particular type of woman only. No redheads, no blondes, no slender model-types. I never try to kiss any of these girls and they appreciate that.

Each day with Severu drives me into the arms of at least one soft, fleshy whore who can take rough handling. As the brutality of my days intensifies so does the need for release. I find salvation in the violent, punishing sex.

My payment has to include their earnings for a day of recovery, but all the women claim they're willing to meet with me again. That's because I'm not deliberately cruel with them, I'm simply driven mad by lust and bloodlust.

Welcome to America

Deplaning after almost nine hours we all feel invigorated, excited to be in America.

Looking around one of the men loudly exclaims *New York is great!* only to be told by the flight attendant: "This is New Jersey, we're at Teterboro Airport. New York is another 100 kilometers that way."

We all turn to look where she's pointing. I didn't see much of her on the flight. She spent most of it with Benet in the bedroom of the private jet.

I'm surprised at her sarcastic tone but the flight crew is American and I wonder *maybe this is their normal way of talking?* I can see that Benet isn't impressed either. He smacks her hard on her butt and pushes her back inside the cabin before continuing down the stairs.

Bulky men wearing shoulder holsters stand beside three identical black town cars idling in wait. Benet and Marcel go to the middle one and gesture for me to join them.

The rest of the men find seats in the front and back cars and then the motorcade heads out. Each of us is given a packet with forged paperwork using our real names. We've got passports, international driving licences, insurance certificates, and bank accounts. We study our information before placing the appropriate documents in pockets and wallets.

The three of us are able to stretch our legs out as we settle in the comfortable seats. Marcel offers cigars but Benet says *no, not in the car.* Marcel is Arnaud's second-in-command, and a very close friend to the kingpin, but he defers to the younger man. Benet is the heir. Marcel has been loaned to us for four or five days to help get our venture set up.

The two of them talk about where we'll be staying, who we plan to meet with, and which of *Les Requins* associates we'll need to contact. Traffic is heavy, although we're driving on the toll highway, and the trip takes almost two hours.

Both Benet and Marcel have dropped off to sleep but I'm wide awake, too interested in seeing all the new sights to close my tired eyes.

New York City is fascinating. I'm overwhelmed by the myriad of smells: seawater, perfume, car exhausts; and noises: construction drills, klaxon horns, and voices shouting in a dozen different languages. The colors, the flashing neon lights, the yellow cabs darting across the lanes, but most of all the many, many people.

People of all races wearing a variety of fashion, uniforms, and native costumes, the locals hurrying and the tourists gawking. All these bodies are oppressive in this muggy heat. The whole experience is one of sensory overload for me, and it seems everyone shares my discomfort.

On our second night a contact of Arnaud in Marseille invites us as VIP guests to the grand opening of his new nightclub. Ricky can't come because his brother Henri, who he had to bring with him, is too young to get in. And there's no way he's going to leave a fourteen-year-old on his own in a strange city.

The fake IDs we were given make us all legal age although some guys, like me, aren't twenty-one yet. Back home I was sneaking into bars two years before reaching our legal age of eighteen so I find American laws strange. *At seventeen a boy can join the armed forces but can't have a drink until four years later? that's crazy.*

Of course Henri sulks because he really is just a kid. Alain, the peacemaker of our gang, suggests: "What about catching a real American baseball game? I've always heard about *Shea Stadium* so–"

Laughing, Antoine interrupts to say: "You're not much of a baseball fan if you don't know *Shea Stadium* shut down twenty years ago or something like that." At Alain's look of dismay he continues: "The New York Mets have got a new home, well it's not new anymore, called *Citi Field*. The Yankees still play at *Yankee Stadium*. I'd love to see a live game, I don't care which team is playing, so sure let's go."

"Great, so that's us three for baseball. Does anybody else want to come? I know Benet and Marcel can't refuse the nightclub invitation but..."

"I'll come with you guys," says Antoine. "I don't want to go clubbing without my wife." The rest of us all tease him for being pussy-whipped but he's still a newlywed. Once we get sorted and settled in a place of our own his wife Jeanne will be flying out to join us. Alain has a common-law wife but Lucie still hasn't decided if she wants to move here or not.

Marcel looks at us and counting out loud says: "Okay then, that's me, Benet, Antal, André, and Georges for the nightclub, while you four go watch a game, right?"

We nod and my group separates to go get ready for our night on the town. Benet and Marcel will probably wear suits but I don't own one so I just put on my jeans with a nice white shirt. When I come back into the main room Benet, dressed up in a suit like I expected, asks: "Don't you have a jacket?"

"I have a sports jacket but I don't need it in this heat," I reply.

"What about uh... you know, protection?"

With a smirk I answer: "Oh don't worry, I'm always armed."

He looks me over and realizes whatever I'm carrying is concealed in my pockets. Actually my gun is strapped around my ankle and my knife is held in a special sheath that lays hidden under my belt. But I do keep my brass knuckles in my pocket.

He grins back at me before turning to the guys to say: "And here I thought Antal wore baggy jeans because he didn't want anyone ogling his tight ass!" Even I have to laugh at that, especially when I see that he's made sullen Henri crack a smile, too.

The five of us go in one car and when the driver pulls up in front of a brightly lit building we see a long line of partygoers outside. I'm not accustomed to VIP treatment so exiting the car and waltzing straight past all the waiting people is a new, but exhilarating, experience. Marcel exchanges a few words with the bouncer who nods respectfully and ushers us inside.

Stepping into the big room with it's flashing lights and loud music I'm immediately reminded of the rave with um.... Charlotte! that was her name. I never did any drinking or dancing at that bar, the whole night took an unexpected turn.

We're handed off to another bouncer-type except this one is wearing a tuxedo. He leads us upstairs past an *Invitation Only* sign to a roped-off section on the second floor.

There are several separate areas formed by suede couches arranged to give each group privacy. We also get a good view of the dance floor below and the nearly naked dancers in glass cages suspended from the ceiling which are at our eye-level. The girls, all of them beautiful, sway seductively in their impossibly high heels while their thong bikinis hide practically nothing.

The only thing that drags my eyes away from them is the gorgeous woman who greets us with the announcement that she will be our server this evening. She speaks with an accent, it sounds like she's from one of the Slavic European countries, and says her name is Callie.

Callie is a stunning blonde wearing nothing but skintight boy shorts that mold to her pussy. I've never actually seen a topless waitress before and I can't help staring. She's dusted some kind of sparkly powder across her perfect tits. They're too full to be called perky but those hard nipples are definitely welcoming. I think we're all feeling awkward and tongue-tied.

Except for Marcel, that is. The older man gives Callie's boobs an appreciative onceover then orders three bottles of champagne. When Callie leaves to fetch the wine her back view shows how well her lovely behind fills out those shorts. Just watching her walk is a treat.

She returns with another two women, equally beautiful and dressed in the same outfit of only shorts and heels. All three are carrying ice-buckets with the champagne. There's lots of laughter and bouncing breasts as they uncork the bottles. As soon as the drinks are poured we're joined by a couple of men who are obviously Russian.

We all stand for the introductions to our hosts and then the men sit facing Benet and Marcel. Each of them pulls a girl onto his lap while gesturing for Callie to slide onto Benet's knee. I'm envious, but grateful that at least my loose jeans hide my hard cock.

It's fun to watch Benet squirm trying to look away from the ripe tits that are practically in his face. His eyes keep getting drawn back to those luscious boobs even as he converses with the two Bratva men who own the club. And the girls too, I imagine.

Marcel tell Georges, André, and I that we're free to go join the crowd on the dance-floor *to try our luck*. One of the men says something in his own language and the girls giggle. I can understand him, though.

When I grew up plenty of people, including my mother, still spoke Russian even though Hungary was freed from the Iron Curtain before

I was born. I don't let on because the words are insulting and I decide it's better to act ignorant and learn what I can.

Callie points out that I'm handsome and they all turn to look at me with one of the men grudgingly agreeing that *maybe that one will have a chance to get laid tonight.* They're far less complimentary about my companions. I'm careful to avoid anyone's eye which is easy with all the bare tits to stare at.

I get up to follow Georges and André back down the stairs where we're quickly absorbed into a sea of writhing bodies and smiling faces. I figure at least half the place is high on Ecstasy.

I can dance well enough not to feel self-conscious and soon find my hand grabbed and my arm stroked by a cute redhead with freckles and a mass of curly hair. When she looks up into my face her eyes widen with interest. When the tip of her tongue peeks out between full lips I'm interested too.

I pull her close and she wiggles her body into an even tighter fit. Reaching her hand up behind my head she pulls me down to shout in my ear *I'm Bridgette.* I answer *Antal.* Her nose wrinkles and I repeat my name until she suddenly nods and calls out *Andal* which is close enough for me.

I spin her until I can place her with her back against my front and we continue to dance as I rub my cock against her hot little body. Instead of leaning away she grinds her ass back into me and I'm trying to figure out if she's a hooker or just one of these free-spirited American girls we hear so much about.

After six solid days of torturing, being tortured, and hate-fucking under Severu's watch it's a relief to know I can still have a normal reaction to a normal encounter. I do want to fuck this pretty little ginger and sure,

I'm imagining how easily I could mark her milky skin with bites and bruises but I don't *have* to hurt her to get off.

Seeing all the naked flesh on display in this nightclub has turned me on just like it should. I'm a healthy young guy who is eager to enjoy the wet, welcoming embrace of a willing cunt. And Bridgette sure acts like she's willing.

Little Bridgette tilts her head back to give me a delightfully wicked look while capturing her bottom lip between small white teeth. *You are fucking edible!* I tell her. Unfortunately I say it in Hungarian because I have no clue how to say it in English. No matter, she hunches her shoulders and gives a mock shiver in appreciation of my deep growling voice. I learned well from watching Severu stoke up Charlotte's fire.

Bridgette reclaims my hand and drags me off the dance floor and into a gloomy hallway. It's the opposite direction from the restrooms so there's no one around. The corridor ends with an emergency fire exit but she stops before we get to it and pushing herself against the wall she reaches up to snake her arms around my neck.

Although she's a plump, curvy package I can easily lift Bridgette up until she wraps her legs around my waist. Holding her in place I quickly free my cock then groan when she insists *condom!* She's right, of course. I have no idea if I'm clean or not but dammit I don't have a rubber. She laughs at the look of chagrin on my face before producing one. *Oh my sweet and sassy slut*, I breathe thankfully, *you are a treasure!*

I quickly sheath my cock and pulling her thong to the side stroke my dick over her wetness. I tickle her clit and her head falls back against the wall. Pushing myself in with a deep thrust I use both hands to grip her soft ass as a handle.

Thinking of Callie's amazing tits I bite at Bridgette's top until she understands and releases one hand from my neck to pull her boobs free of her bra. Ah, yes! I knew her skin would be that shade of white so white there's a hint of blue in the flesh. She holds up a nipple to my mouth and I suck hard, grazing the nubbin with my teeth just enough so she can feel it. She likes that and is quick to switch over to feed me her other nipple. I give it the loving attention it's due.

I'm not in the least bit inclined to hurt this girl, I don't want to, I'm just focused on giving us both as much pleasure as possible. Later on, in a rare moment of self-analysis, I decide I must have responded in kind to her generous, uncomplicated attitude towards sex. Her no-strings-attached, in-the-moment, lusty need called to me in a way I hadn't felt since I was a young teen having his first experience.

Like all the wolves in my pack I was introduced to sex through a ritual involving Omegas in heat, but we also freely enjoyed sexual play with the she-wolves. Both the males and females were especially randy if we could catch them during a run.

Bridgette came, but I hold back until she's ready to cum again so we can both orgasm together. We put our clothing back together and I take her to the bar, wanting to buy her a drink, but she just shakes her head *no thanks!*

I watch with a smile as she dances away from me back into the crowd of happy bodies gyrating to the heavy bass beat. She doesn't look back.

Returning to the VIP section I sat down and threw back a glass of champagne, wanting it for the cold liquid rather than the alcohol. The two Russian men have left and Marcel is gone as well. Callie and the other two servers are also gone but from the lazy smile on Benet's face I know he's at least gotten a blow job.

Thinking of how easily these waitresses display their tits to every man in the VIP Lounge makes me want to grab Callie and hurt her. I don't know why, but I have the urge to see her crying with snot and spit and make-up running down her face. Making her ugly as she draws in loud, sobbing breaths. It's actually impossible for that girl to look ugly but I want to see her degraded, humiliated, and frightened.

Just then she returns, alone, carrying a cigar box that she offers first to Benet and then to me. We both decline and that makes her frown. I effortlessly lift her up to straddle me and glance over her shoulder at Benet for permission. He gives me a wry smile and gestures for me to *go ahead.*

I take hold of Callie's beautiful boobs and knead them. Her nipples are hard enough to poke into the palms of my hands. I squeeze and when I manhandle her too roughly she bites back a gasp of pain, pretending to love what I'm doing.

The deception makes me feral and I continue to massage knowing how strongly my fingers are gripping. I squish her tits together and rub my face into her cleavage. I'm sure my five o'clock shadow feels like sandpaper on her tender skin.

I push Callie off my lap onto the floor until she's obediently kneeling before me. I can see relief in her eyes but that won't last long. Holding tightly to the hair close to her scalp I keep her in place until I free my cock and press it into her mouth.

She immediately opens wide and begins sucking and licking, making fake sounds of appreciation which infuriate me even more. I stand, lifting her up off her haunches and begin to ruthlessly fuck her face without caring that anyone up here can see us.

Benet has been watching all long and now I can sense some other men leaning in and even coming closer to see better. I don't know whether or not she likes having an audience and I don't care.

I push myself past her tongue and into her throat. She gags, but I don't let up. When her eyes start streaming I pull back enough to let her gulp some air and then I'm thrusting deep down her gullet again. When I cum she has no choice but to swallow every drop even while her face is turning red. I pull my cock out and taking in the sight of Callie's wet, red eyes and fingermarked tits I feel a great sense of satisfaction at her degradation.

Reaching into my pocket I grab a handful of bills but Benet tells me *no need, she's on the house.*

"Sweet," I reply before wrapping her fingers around the money and clearly saying in Russian: "Here's a tip for good service, pretty whore."

Benet claps when he hears the words even if he doesn't understand the meaning. Then laughing he stands and throws his arm across my shoulders as we head for the stairs leaving beautiful Callie crying with humiliation.

This time I'm the one who doesn't look back.

On the third day Benet and Marcel gather the crew in a small restaurant that gives us privacy. Standing, Benet makes the announcement: "We're not staying here in New York."

The short statement has the men all exchanging glances. Since I was already aware of what the boss was going to say I'm studying the faces around me.

While Benet explains that the opportunities in New York City are spread too thin, the territories are too small, and there's constant battling among the many gangs for supremacy, I watch to make sure all the men are in agreement with the boss. New York's heightened air of feverish activity is very exciting but also overstimulating to us newcomers.

The plan is to relocate right across the country to the West Coast. When someone cheers saying *California!* Benet shakes his head answering *Nope, but next door to it.*

I unfold the map I've been given and the men lean in to see the red spot I'm tapping. Oceanport, Oregon right on the coastline.

Benet explains that they chose Oceanport because it has a population of only 8,000 which means no competition to fight over our market. Most of *Les Requins* income comes from dealing drugs.

I draw a line with my finger and the crew follows the route showing that Oceanport is conveniently located on the 101 Highway with direct access to Highway 20. This meets Interstate 5 leading up to Salem, the capital.

"If it's right there on top of California it must have the same kind of weather, *non*?" asks Ricky.

"Not the dry sunshine. It's mild, not hot-hot, and rainy. Well we're told it rains frequently all along the coast. Further inland it's much drier.

The main industry is commercial fishing. They've got a small Sheriff's office, plus there's Oregon State Police which also serves as highway patrol."

"And the FBI," puts in André.

"Not in Oceanport, and not even in the closest city which is Newport. The FBI are in Salem and Portland and a few other cities, though. There are biker gangs and crime syndicates all along the West Coast but, again, not in Oceanport. It's pristine territory for us."

I note that all the men respond favorably to the move which is good news for the cohesiveness of the gang. It only needs one malcontent to poison the camaraderie of the crew and the respect vital for effective leadership.

These men are ready and willing to venture out and support our operation. It's a good omen for our fresh start. If anyone is disappointed at leaving New York City behind they aren't saying so.

We discuss travel arrangements and learn a contact of *Les Requins* is already scouting out a safe house for us to base our business out of. We'll deal with vehicles and housing one we're acclimated to the new place. Buying locally as much as we can will establish good relations with our neighbors.

I can't safely phone home to Hungary, but someone traveling to Romania will stop at our compound en route to give my news to Gyuri.

Les Petits Requins

Our gang, *Les Petits Requins [The Little Sharks]*, thrives in Oregon. The men in the ranks put down roots in our small city by forming friendships, marrying local girls, and sponsoring kids' sports teams. Outwardly we're all Americanized but we keep our social circle small, restricted to members of our organization. No one is joining the Rotary Club although we're happy to support their fundraising events.

The Sheriff isn't a stupid man, he's aware that we are a criminal association, but he can't act without complaints, and we're careful not to give him cause.

The Frenchies, as we get called by the locals, introduced ourselves by buying a rundown tavern to fix up. We earned our credentials by transforming it with hospitality, hiring locally, serving good food, and showcasing live music on Saturday nights.

"You know, lots of bands and singers are auditioning for spots Boss, so how come we don't have live music on Fridays, too?" asks Henri. Even though Henri is too young to be a member of the crew he's Ricky's dependent and part of our family so the guys indulge him.

Benet smiles at the teen explaining: "Saturday night is for couples, it's date night, and they come for the music and dancing. Fridays are for singles and those married folk who take off their wedding bands and pretend they're single. That kind doesn't appreciate a band and won't even listen, they just want to find a hook-up. It's also *boys'* – and *girls'* – *night out* and those customers just want to drink rounds of shooters and get rowdy."

"Bet they wanna hook-up, too" replies in Henri with a big grin. His brother cuffs him on the head, but good-naturedly, saying *don't even think about it kid, not for a couple more years.*

We've renamed the bar *The French Connection*. None of us ever heard of the Best Picture winner by that name or we might have avoided associating the club with illegal drug trafficking. By time we find out Benet and I can only shrug and chuckle at the irony.

The locals quickly adopt it as *a good place for dinner* and it becomes a popular spot all week long. Benet makes a point of circulating among the clientele and when the older crowd laugh and repeat the phrase *we come from France* he asks one of them to explain.

"It's a line from an old Saturday Night Live skit. See, this family of aliens is trying to blend in like humans and whenever they do something outer-spacey they explain it away by saying in their funny monotone voices *we come from France*."

Benet laughs along with the man but has no idea why anyone thinks that's funny, deciding that *Americans are weird*. Someday he'll move back to France but there's no need to share that plan with anyone here.

The Little Sharks are in the drug trade but we don't do business in Oceanport. While it remains our base of operations, the drugs we deal are sold at the three dozen colleges within a 100-mile radius.

Nine or ten years earlier Oregon legalized recreational marijuana but there's always an appetite for more potent weed than what the State allows. Our gang quickly expanded our market with the recent decriminalization of cocaine and heroin in small amounts.

Our investment in the bar, and the other local nightlife venues we back, gives us enough control to keep drugs out of our town. The DEA has no reason to come sniffing around.

Benet's leadership of the gang has been equitable and profitable, earning him respect and loyalty from his men. As a result my job as the enforcer and interrogator is relatively easy. Most of my work is straightening out incomers trying to encroach on our territory. I make sure they don't try again.

I burn up a lot of my energy by working out for hours each day. Benet and I start each morning with a five-mile run before breakfast. The two of us are well-built, healthy young men who enjoy competing. When we walk into the bar everyone notices, and most of the customers know us. We have our pick of the women, and none of the men ever try to pick a fight.

A decade later a girl will tell me that I've got t*he Big Dick Energy of a typical Alpha-hole* and by then I'm arrogant enough to be flattered.

Marcel returned to Marseille which meant I've taken on a more active role as Benet's second-in-command. I enjoy the planning and strategizing, but find the day-to-day duties of leadership boring.

After a year of living in Oceanport I hear from Gyuri that the warrant for my arrest has been rescinded and I'm no longer a wanted man. He tells me I'm free to come back home to Hungary. The assault charge was dropped when the case against me collapsed, withdrawn by the complainant Beáta. I know that Beáta is now married to Kada. She's my sister-in-law, a member of my family and pack. I can't say how I feel about that because... I really don't feel anything. Not anger, but also not forgiveness.

It's a revelation to me that I no longer want to return and live in Hungary. The bitterness I experienced when I was forced away from my home and homeland dissipated in the comfortable new life I found in the States. I don't feel like an American yet, but there's no yearning to return to Europe.

Still, Gyuri's news is a relief. I'm now free to contact various families in order to expand and build lucrative connections in Eastern Europe. I'd like to see the gang move away from the drug trade where the wars are a constant and deadly threat. Instead I've begun fostering partnerships with arms dealers who are eager to branch out overseas.

With this new business and our local distribution network the gang is busy and prosperous. Benet and I still live in the same safe house the gang acquired when we first came here. The two us have grown into a close friendship with neither of us choosing wives.

Me because I'm not interested in female companionship outside of paid-for sex. Whores are easier than pick-ups who want to turn one-night stands into something more.

Benet likes to have fun but never lets it get serious. He knows someday he'll be recalled to Marseille and when that happens he'll marry a French girl, probably to strengthen an alliance for the gang.

In the meantime he keeps himself busy *playing the field* as they say here. I've discovered the Americans use baseball terms for a lot of their slang and colloquialisms. Just another reason why I don't think I'll ever master this peculiar language.

Most of the thoughts in my head never find their way to my mouth because I don't want to look or sound stupid. The funny part is that people think my silence means I'm thoughtful and clever. Or else I'm *the strong silent type.* That's what one girl told me.

Girls spend a lot of their time talking to me. I know it's only 'cause of my looks, it's not like they know me or anything. Women enjoy the chase just as much as men do, maybe more because even when we're chasing after them they're still the ones directing the game.

When we're out socializing I'll dance with any girls who ask me and kiss the ones who say it's their birthday, but I don't date. Benet teases me saying *I need a good girl who knows how to have sexy fun instead of spending all my money on prostitutes just to get laid.*

He saw how I was with Callie back at that nightclub in New York City but he didn't understand, hell I can barely figure out why I acted the way I did. All I know for sure is that I like hurting women while I fuck them and I don't want to do that to somebody nice.

I enjoyed the sex I had with that girl Bridgette but she was one-of-a-kind and it was only ever going to be a one-off.

I just tell Benet that *things never get complicated with hookers. Nobody falls in love and nobody falls pregnant.* He understands about that since he's had to extricate himself from a couple of tricky situations.

We're building a good business and a good life here but some day he'll have to go back to France. Plenty of time to settle down then.

Several years have passed, our lives are progressing smoothly, and now that day has come.

It's just before 9:00 am and fresh from showering after my morning run I sit down to join the men for breakfast. Nodding greetings I help myself from the platter of bacon and eggs when the boss's cellphone rings.

One of the first thing the gang decided when we arrived in America was to learn and speak English. This has always been difficult for me. Although I can understand and speak the languages of Eastern Europe I struggled to learn French, and find English so much worse. My understanding of the language far surpasses my ability to speak it so I don't. That's how I got to be known as a quiet, reflective man.

Looking at the caller's name Benet answers the phone by saying: "*Allô [Hello]* ?" which makes me stop eating so I can listen. I give all my attention to Benet's side of the conversation and his reaction to this call from France. Benet is silent, tense and frowning, while the caller speaks at length.

59

His face crumples over the bad news he's hearing then clears his throat and asks *when? how?* and *do we know who?* He listens some more and then fires off a few sentences, too rapid for me to understand, before nodding and ending the call. The fingers of his hand holding the phone are rigid with strain.

He takes a deep breath then tells us: "My father has just been killed, assassinated by the Romanians," he lays out the facts as he knows them.

"Those bastards have been pushing and pushing into our territory and brazenly attacked one of our restaurants. That was Marcel, he got shot too, but it's minor and he's coping," here Benet breaks off to compose himself.

"Marcel was crying, not from the bullet but because of losing my father. It's hard to hear an older man cry... he said Dad was killed instantly. They'd just arrived at the restaurant, they'd come early in order to have a meeting before their meal. They must have been followed because the shooting started almost immediately–"

Interrupting I say: "Or they have a rat who contacted the killers to say where they were."

"Yeah, well, that will be up to us to find out." Benet places his hand over his mouth, gripping his chin, and pressing his fingers tight against his lips. But I can hear his broken whisper of *mon père, mon père [my father]*. He's struggling.

This news means he has to return to Marseille right away in order to fill the void in *Les Requins* leadership.

He and I have talked many times about the eventuality of this day, but living comfortably in the States made it seem like some far-off event.

It's easy to imagine that time stands still at the place we left behind. That the streets will look the same, that people we know won't age, and that no one dies. It's a shock to both of us to have to face up to it now. Our lives and our world have been irrevocably changed.

"Antal, *mon ami [my friend]*, I know you have no ties to Marseille and you're content here in Oregon so I wonder... I wonder if you are willing to take over this operation? To run *Les Petits Requins* for me here?"

"Benet thank you, you honor me, but you don't need to make any decisions now. I will look after this business while you go back and get things sorted. Marcel and Severu will help you. Maybe there's someone else, one of your brothers or some other family member who might be better suited to take over here? I don't know, but we don't need to figure that out right now.

I'll take charge here and once you've crushed those Romanian fuckers you'll have a clear mind to decide what comes next."

The two of us set in motion the plans we previously made. A private jet is hired for the trip and Benet packs up most of his stuff. He won't be returning for some time, and then it will only be to visit.

We share signing authority on the business accounts, and the managers of our legitimate businesses already report to either me or Benet, so our work can continue without interruption. I'm ready, though reluctant, to step in to my temporary role as gang leader.

Benet stays in Marseille. He's walked right into a violent turf war there and a lot of blood is shed over the next couple of years.

Les Petits Requins end up splitting the illegal enterprise three ways. The growth in drug sales at the colleges is enough to justify dividing that business into two units. These will be overseen by two of the original members, Ricky and André, who have become permanent residents. I elect to stay in the US as well, managing the distribution of arms.

"Besides," Benet tells me during one of our calls, "I don't speak any of those Eastern languages so I can't deal with those Russian types. They'll just rob me blind."

He and I amicably decide to end our association although we will always keep our friendship. On the whirlwind trips that Benet makes to Oregon from time to time the two us always make a point of getting together.

To help make a clean break from *Les Petits Requins* I decide to leave Oceanport and move further down the coast into Northern California. There I buy a home where I live alone, with day staff coming in.

I've become a wealthy man running an independent illegal business that isn't tied to a particular location.

I know my reputation is mixed in our criminal society. My skill-set in brutal cruelty, acquired as Severu's protégé, aids me in negotiating with the vicious element that deals in the sale and transport of armaments. It also gets me contracts as an independent interrogator where I have a high success rate.

I'm also known to be violent towards the sex workers I hire but also generous, probably overly so, and I never maim or cause lasting damage to the working girls. I realize they're often frightened by me because they've no way of knowing just how far I'll go. Especially when I produce a knife or semi-strangle them.

I haven't shifted once since leaving Europe and I've lived in America for several years now. I'm 24 years old.

Unleashing the Beast

The door is closed quietly but Agneta's been listening for it and is ready. She eases out of her room just in time to see the silhouette of a tall, well-built man disappearing down the stairs.

Now that he's gone her anxious waiting is over. She runs next door and pulls Mimi into her arms breathless with concern.

"Mimi, sweetheart, did he hurt you? Of course he did that's what he paid for. Fuck! I wish you'd never agreed. Honey, open your eyes and look at me," she demands.

Taking a deep breath the crying girl insists: "I'm all right really Netty. I mean yeah, it hurts, but it's not too bad. Nothing broken, anyhow." The smile she attempts is lopsided. Agneta takes one look at Mimi's puffy, swollen lips and bursts into tears.

Mimi huffs a laugh saying: "Oh great, now you're crying too! Really I'm okay."

"But he hit you, your lips are all—"

"No, no he didn't. He never hit me at all this is... well, he got a bit overstimulated and was rough when he fucked my mouth."

"Omigod, Mimi." Agneta swipes at the tears under her eyes and then gently kisses her lover's face. They hug silently, comforting each other. Mimi has just entertained Antal as a client and her whole body is sore and aching.

"I hate that you saw him again when he leaves you like this."

"But look how much money he gave me!" exclaims Mimi, grabbing up the wad of bills left on the bed. "Here take it to hide."

"We can't take it, the bitch knows he always tips and she'll be in soon enough demanding her share."

Pressing the cash into Agneta's hand Mimi begs: "Please, Netty. Take some at least. The bitch doesn't deserve any of it."

"She sure doesn't. We know she's charging him extra 'cause of how he is and what he does and that's still not enough for the bitch." Agneta takes half of the tip money which still leaves a sizable amount. Her bra is too sheer to hide anything so she slips the bills into her thong and sits down.

A couple of minutes later the door is flung open and the Madame marches in with her hand outstretched. She finds Mimi held in Agneta's arms being cuddled and soothed. The wad of bills is back lying on the bed and the Madame snatches it up, counting, before taking more than half of it.

"That's Mimi's money! it's her tip and she earned it!" Agneta protests indignantly.

"Huh! look at her, she's useless to me for at least one day, maybe two."

"Yeah and you've already charged him for her time off–"

Interrupting the Madame declares: "He pays for the income I'll lose, this will pay her room-and-board while she isn't earning."

Pleased at having the last word the greedy woman tips up her chin and leaves clutching the money she's stolen. She doesn't regret her actions. Once upon a time she'd been the one forced to lie on her back day after day for all those faceless men. She only survived it by hardening her heart and vowing to always take care of herself first.

Left alone again Agneta makes Mimi lie down on the bed so she can check her over. The girl's eyes are red from crying and her neck and shoulders are marked with bites. Bruises are blossoming across her breasts right down to her belly, hips, and thighs. Agneta picks up a bottle of *Witch Hazel* and smooths it over Mimi's discolored skin.

"It looks like he used you as a punching bag!"

"No, no I told you. He didn't hit me, he never does."

"Well he must have used his belt to spank you because your poor bum is really red and it's badly bruised."

"No, he doesn't spank or hit or anything like that... well, he does slap a bit you know, he'll slap my tits or my ass or thigh. But he never actually punches me, he just grabs hold and squeezes really hard with his hands, his fingers are so long and strong, and he grips so tight."

"You know what they say about men with long fingers," Agneta tries to joke but her jealousy surfaces and she scowls.

"Well in Antal's case that's true! but don't make faces at me. He doesn't use his long cock to give me any pleasure. Believe me it's punishment the way he drives in deeper and deeper. He's like one of those pneumatic drills you hear construction workers use brrrrrr-brrrrrr-brrrrrr over and over again," she has to growl out the sound because she can't vibrate her lips. Agneta is mollified and gently kisses and caresses her friend with tenderness.

When Mimi puts her arms around Agneta's neck and lifts herself up her lover spots blood smeared on the sheet.

"What's this? Are you cut? you were bleeding, let me see!" Turning Mimi on her side the two look at the thin cuts on the side of her body, under her armpit. "He used a knife on you? That fucker! You won't be seeing him again," Agneta insists.

"Oh Netty, I didn't even notice the cutting and it's already clotted. They're just shallow cuts, like paper cuts–"

"Paper cuts really hurt!"

"Well I don't remember it happening. We must have been fucking at the time and I was probably facing away from him."

Agneta groans at the thought of her friend being abused this way. "Oh Mimi, please, promise you won't see him again."

"I can't, Netty. Look at all the money we've got, even after the bitch has taken her cut. But listen there's no point arguing about it because he might not come back. The bitch said he usually doesn't, that I'm the only one here he's ever asked for twice."

* * *

The first time I was sent to this hooker's room I almost rejected the girl on sight. She matched all of my requirements perfectly except she wasn't white, she was Asian. From behind she looked just like Beáta but face-on the difference was obvious.

The mixed blood in her body gives her eyes an upward tilt, forms full lips, and curls her hair into luxuriant waves. She's an exotic beauty. Despite the race issue I got turned on, and once I started using her body I was hooked.

I think her name is Mimi or Miriam, something like that. In my own mind I call all of these women *this-Beáta*.

This girl cries so prettily even as she takes the abuse I inflict. She gets bitten, groped, pinched, twisted, and slapped, and gracefully submits to everything I do. When I mercilessly rub her clit for lubrication she even orgasms.

With my eyes closed I can still picture Beáta while I'm ravaging this girl's soft, pliant flesh. Of course I never heard my teenaged lover whimper or cry, I was always gentle with her, but I can imagine how she would sound and pretend it's her in my hands.

I broke my own rule when I asked for that same girl on my next visit to the whorehouse. Predictably the Madame made a fuss about how much it cost her to lose such a popular girl while she recovered from the damage... but I cut her off by saying *just tell me how much.*

After our business was transacted the Madame escorted me to the girl's room warning her to be sure to keep me happy.

A thrill runs through me as I see how her eyes widen and how she nervously nibbles her bottom lip at the sight of me. It's clear she recalls my last visit with perfect clarity, remembering how my bestiality frightened her. I'm ready to snarl and growl as I bite and paw her again, like I'm some unhinged, feral animal.

Knowing the girl is terrified stimulates my demons. I give her a closed-mouth smile keeping my face impassive, but I'm sure lust sparks in my eyes.

Stalking towards the bed my excitement grows as she backpedals, trying to get away. Now I show my teeth in a ferocious grin and she freezes, helpless and at my mercy. My cock is so hard I worry that I'm gonna injure myself if I wait a second longer. I squeeze it firmly and quickly roll on a condom.

Grabbing hold of the girl's ankles I yank her legs apart and rub the head of my cock against her folds. She isn't aroused when I drive into her and her grunts of pain at the abrupt intrusion are so satisfying to hear.

I fuck her steadily but pull out before cumming and force my cock down her throat. Her face, already wet with tears, is now shiny with saliva and phlegm as she struggles to breathe. She's an absolute vision.

I grip her chin and pinch her bottom lip as leverage while I face-fuck her hard. I slide out briefly, barely as long as necessary for the girl to drag in a breath, then I plunge back down her throat driving back and forth. When I unload my hot cum I hold onto the blissful moment until she pounds my thigh to pull out and give her air.

Pinning *this Beata* down my hands and mouth rove all over her warm body. I suck and squeeze and bite until her skin is marked with streaks of red. I like to finish my session with anal sex and tell her to get me another condom and some lube.

She fetches the stuff and when I've got her positioned I feel how she's bracing herself for my assault. I rim her butt-hole with my thumb and apply plenty of lube because I like the slippery feeling. I begin by teasing just the head inside her. I rock in and out slowly before giving a hard push to breach that hot little hole.

I keep the nail of my little finger grown long but not to snort coke like some people imagine. No, I keep it filed to a sharp point. I use it now to lightly slice down *this-Beáta's* side. The sight of blood welling up stirs my passion. Catching up a few of the bright red drops on my fingers I lick the tips and groan at the coppery taste.

Cupping the girl's full breasts to massage I bend my head down to suck on the back of her neck. She makes cooing sounds as pleasant sensations thrill through her body. She detaches her mind from the pain and concentrates on her building orgasm, murmuring encouragement and instruction. *Oh yes, just there, yes right there. Just like that now faster, faster.*

She isn't aware that her hand has slid down to rub her clit while slipping one and then two fingers inside herself. When she bucks her hips in an orgasmic spasm I find myself shouting out something unintelligible and hugging her so tightly she struggles for breath.

I slowly pull out of her stretched butt-hole and tie off the condom. The two of us lay panting, sore and satiated. I rise and look down at the girl's curvy body, bruises already forming to mar her smooth skin. It makes me feel almost affectionate.

I'm not ashamed of the monster I unleash through sex. It's just the way I am. Since I'm not angry with myself I don't need to transfer any feelings of contempt or disgust onto the girl. I know some men are embarrassed to use hookers, but I don't know why they feel that way.

I pull on my jeans, I didn't bother removing my shirt, and reaching into the front pocket pull out a fistful of money. I don't count it, I just place it on the bed without a word.

Leaving, I close the door quietly behind myself. I might return to *this-Beáta* again... but probably not.

Rescuing the Orphans

From what I've seen and heard most Americans don't like shifters. I know this antipathy is based out of fear and ignorance about the unknown. Humans fear our bestial nature and fear our physical supremacy. People are always wary of anything or anyone different or strange. It's human nature. Humans really are quite weak beings. I guess that's why they're so quick to lash out.

The police, in particular, have no sympathy for us. They profile shifters and are always ready to accuse and blame. Although I stopped shifting I'm still a shifter and always will be. I'm not a werewolf, I have control over my ability to shift and can do so at any time of day or night. The full moon does stir my lusty urge to rut but I feel that way even in my human form. The moon affects us all.

There's been a lot of news lately about the growing movement to outlaw shifters, particularly wolves, from society, sequestering us in our own area. A ghetto or a reservation. Maybe they'd like to exile us to Guantanamo Bay?

California seems to be okay but then this is an *anything goes* kind of place. Still, I'm not taking any chances. I've suppressed my wolf since before Marseilles. His sadness seeps into my bones but by keeping him locked away I'm protecting us both.

So I'm angry to discover that killings in this area are being attributed to a rogue pack. It's drawing unwanted police attention and that threatens my business. The attacks are happening at hospitals, convents, homeless shelters, any place with easy access to a large number of the defenseless.

News reports vary, but the consensus is that there are six or seven shifters behind these cowardly attacks on the vulnerable. The massacres are so savage there's worry the animals are rabid.

Once again the media is full of talking heads discussing segregation and interviewing the man on the street for a snapshot of public opinion. It isn't good.

By deliberate choice I've had no contact with the shifter community but I need to know more about this renegade crew. I start visiting known shifter bars trying to pick up information.

Tales are whispered but it's obvious no one has direct knowledge. I've heard rumors at several locations that the local orphanage is the next target. It sounds plausible, and now I just have to find out when.

I'm in one of the shifter bars when a group of young men, as many as ten of them, come in looking for trouble. The youths are big-built, big enough to be players on a football team. They're college-age and bring their mission of *righting wrongs* full of confidence.

They talk of preventing the next tragedy by *stopping the werewolves before tomorrow's full moon*. Inevitably a fight breaks out but I always travel with bodyguards and we're able to subdue the boys before anyone in the place actually shifts.

It's a close thing, though. I can feel the hot, primal need surging around me. The air is thick with lupine pheromones and my craving for that scent makes me lightheaded.

Believing I now know the date I take my crew to stake-out the streets surrounding the orphanage. It's an old building built of adobe bricks in the Spanish Mission style. Once pink it's now faded to almost white and looks ghostly in this evening's fog. Maybe there's enough cloud cover to hide the moon when it peaks?

Except I know shifters don't need a full moon to shift, and werewolves aren't sane enough to form a pack with an objective. I suspect this gang is playing up the myth to heighten the fear factor.

As I get close to the building I'm almost overwhelmed by the odor of terror emitted by horrified humans. The shifters must be here! Rallying my men we launch our attack, catching the invaders from behind. The wolves are torn between fighting us or carrying forward to sate their bloodlust on the innocent children. In the midst of this wild melee of snapping, snarling wolves I really have to struggle to keep my inner beast under control.

Naturally we've come armed but I prefer the quiet of knives over guns. Shots will bring in the authorities. It's fine for them to show up and deal with the aftermath, but they've proven ineffective in stopping the pack so that's up to us.

With my left hand I crush throats while my right slashes and stabs. Blood spurts from a severed jugular and instead of drinking it down my human self has to wipe it away in pretended disgust.

Inside I'm rejoicing at bathing in the blood of my enemy. The taste and smell of it excites me into a murderous frenzy. I'm in a maelstrom of fighting bodies that blur, everything happening fast, quickly, and deadly.

There are screams of fear and shrieks of pain but the pounding in my veins shoots through my body drowning out other noise. The initial stories are wrong because there are close to two dozen fighting wolves. Maybe the rogue pack has attracted like-minded followers?

I've successfully fought my way right up to a side window and now drag a hairy, muscular body back out through the shards of broken glass. My inner savage is gleeful hearing the monster's agonized cry. Fuck him.

Inside the room I can see another beast clawing at a pair of small legs, trying to pull the kicking child from under a cot. That's the only place showing streaks of blood on the floor so thank Christ we've arrived in time.

All the children are huddled under the cots in this dormitory, clinging together, some wailing, some shouting, some emitting high-pitched whistling shrieks, while the rest are stunned silent. The air full of panic, terror, and the tantalizing odor of urine.

An expert throw of my knife lands a killing blow to the base of the attacking wolf's neck. The animal immediately collapses and the brave little boy scurries back. I can hear shouts of *clear!* coming from the team in the hallway that's made its way into the building from the front door. The marauders were stopped in time. It's good to know something positive came from this manic, frenzied battle.

I knock away the remaining pieces of jagged glass before leaping into the room. First I check that the wolf is dead then I retrieve my knife.

I don't try to speak to the children, they're far too frightened. Instead I sniff for any other wolves before retreating back to the window. My rapid scan of the room is stopped when I meet the arresting gaze of a child maybe ten or eleven years old.

She's a beautiful girl with long platinum-blonde hair and the most stunning aquamarine eyes. The two of us are locked in a stare that raises my neck hair and sends tingles down my spine. It's like time is suspended as I experience a mysterious pull towards this child. It almost feels like a premonition, like I am fated to save this little girl. The sight of her trembling mouth breaks the spell and I quickly exit the room, still feeling dazed.

Contact with the shifters has left me angry and unsettled. Thankfully this wolf pack is now destroyed. The locals think the killing was done by vigilantes and that's good. Still, there's just as much negativity from the humans as before.

I am more determined than ever to keep my wolf tightly controlled. But I sense, regretfully, that this repression thwarts my nature.

Into the Abyss of Depravity

I have a new recurring dream. I still have the old one, the one where I savagely attack Beáta, and it's a nightmare. But now another girl haunts my nights. That girl from the orphanage. The girl with the aquamarine eyes.

I don't dream of harming her, and never anything sexual because she's only a kid. No, in my dream all I can see are her eyes and I get lost in them. In my dream we have a meaningful connection, no words but... it means something. Something important. She's important.

But time passes and the dreams become infrequent. It makes me sad because I always feel better, redeemed and refreshed, after reliving our mysterious wordless encounter. The memory dims as the time between dreams grows longer, until it fades altogether and she's gone from my mind.

My life devolves into a downward spiral of sadistic brutality and vicious violence. I'm employed to kill and kill again because I'm deeply feared and very effective.

I have no soul left, demons have claimed it. I don't feel pleasure or enjoyment in murder but do feel an ongoing need, a compulsion to fulfil some horrific imperative.

It's like there's another Antal taking control of my thoughts and actions, sending me into a fugue state, always craving more. It's not my wolf. My wolf has gone silent after me denying him for so long.

Besides, this other self doesn't have the nobility of a proud, fearless wolf. This other self barely clings to his sanity once he succumbs to the raging fever of bloodlust.

It's taking me a long time to clean up my dungeon after last night's contracted torture session. I was ordered to inflict extreme suffering on the victim before delivering his death. I was on camera so the couple who hired me could watch in real time. I'm sure they got no pleasure from it, just as I know they'll rewatch the video more than once and it will never be enough.

I hid my identity with a black hood that completely covered my head. I knew I couldn't rely on just keeping my face averted from the camera once I got into the zone.

The hood was decorated with a very realistic skull in phosphorescent paint for a menacing look. The anonymity heightened the victim's fear. I'll have to buy more of these hoods, the one I wore is now too bloody to keep. Although... maybe the sight and smell of dried blood will enhance the next victim's terror?

I'm wondering *why am I so completely detached from any remorse over the pain and suffering I cause? Was I born lacking empathy? or have the experiences of my life shaped me this way?* Sadly, I have to admit that I really don't care why.

The victim deserved it but regardless, I don't need to judge him or justify myself, not when my bank account is full.

Of course what this guy did to those two little sisters absolutely merited my most savage brutality and he got it. The walls of this room are sprayed with blood splatter worthy of a *Jackson Pollock* painting, and the floor is a muddy mess of organs and offal. The stench of sweat and shit is more offensive to me than the images in my mind's eye of the pedophile's stripped and shredded flesh.

No, the murdering deviant earned every howl of agony and every shriek of horror I extracted from him. It won't bring closure to the parents, nothing will ever ease their pain, but there is a measure of satisfaction when the scales seem to be balanced.

The woman I called to come service me barely got through the front door before I was on her. I hadn't showered so the man's blood was still on my hands and face, in my hair, and on my clothes. She recoiled and turned to flee but I dragged her down to the floor and there, on the cold marble of my foyer, she submitted to my angry lust.

I pulled hair, squashed handfuls of soft flesh, bit tender skin, and thoroughly fucked all three of her holes. For that I paid triple her overnight fee for less than forty-five minutes of her time. Well worth it to me.

I really must have sold my soul to the devil, I think. *Otherwise surely I'd feel something?*

I'm blank, practically comatose, on the days and nights when I don't have a villain in my basement. I become one of those predators whose life revolves around waiting for the chance to capture unwitting prey. Like a crocodile 90% submerged in the muddy water ready to attack, or a panther crouched high in the trees waiting to pounce, or a coiled snake camouflaged and patiently willing its prey to come closer.

Gyuri still calls me but I rarely answer the phone and never reach out myself. I decided some time ago that the life I had in Hungary is best forgotten. But obliterating my past leaves me living in limbo, I can't see a way forward. I have no future, only this miserable present.

Killing someone else's enemy – cleanly or dreadfully – and afterwards roughly, harshly fucking a well-paid hooker are the only real moments in my bleak existence.

I will later come to learn that this is the direct result of suppressing my true nature, my wolf.

Grigor Brings Solace

Three days. No clients calling, no killing, no fucking. Just nothing but silence and empty spaces of time. When the doorbell rings I ignore it, as usual. No one I know is going to come calling, and I'm in no mood for strangers.

The doorbell is followed up with a polite knock that's soon replaced by impatient pounding. An instant flare of anger propels me to the front entrance. *Fuck the peephole* I think as I yank the door open letting it bounce off the wall.

My frown deepens with shock when I realize I'm looking at Grigor, my Beta from back in Hungary, and once my closest friend. His huge body fills the entryway.

"*Testvér! [Brother]*" he exclaims happily. His massive arms pull me into his special kind of manly embrace laughing loudly and lifting me off my feet.

Breathless I look into his face with wonder stumbling over the words *how? why?* but he doesn't answer with words. He kisses me on each cheek in a traditional greeting before holding my head and gently bumping our foreheads together. I feel my eyes watering with emotion which he ignores, kissing me fully on my mouth. *It's Grigor! He's here, he's really here!*

I hadn't realized how lonely and alone I'd been all this time. Grigor ends the kiss and grins, nudging me backwards to allow him room to step inside my home.

"Come in, come in," I say, turning aside in invitation.

I'm a big bulky man but I forgot how massive Grigor is. His astonishing bulk makes every feature larger than life, starting with his wide smiling mouth.

Four years older than me he's been part of my life since the very beginning, watching over me as a good Beta should.

"Gyuri said he hadn't heard from you for ages so I made him give me your address. I needed to see you for myself, and Antal, you look like shit."

"You traveled a long way to insult me, my friend."

"That's okay, I'm staying. I'll whip you back into shape in no time," he laughs at my expression explaining: "No, I don't mean that kind of whipping although... sure, I can take care of that for you, too."

I start laughing and though it's verging on hysteria Grigor joins in and soon we're both gasping for breath. Wheezing in recovery our eyes lock and that sets us off again. When I finally gain control of myself my face is wet with tears of laughter and something more... loss. I realize I've been speaking in Hungarian for the first time in far too long.

Grigor shakes his head in disbelief when I'm unable to tell him where the closest Turkish Bath is. Muttering under his breath he searches on his phone telling me: "Here they use the real name for the baths, *Hammam,* and we're going now." He drags his couple of suitcases and bags into the entryway and leaves them there urging me to *hurry up.* My arguments are ineffectual as he hustles me out the door.

Hours later we're lying side-by-side, cleansed and relaxed, and now receiving deep tissue massages. It's an all-male environment and the masseurs have punishingly strong fingers that dissolve the tension of tight muscles.

I've been too long without male companionship. I miss Benet and the camaraderie of gang life. I ache for the brotherhood of my pack. Seeing Grigor again reminds me of how much I've lost.

When we're home again Grigor takes me to bed where he holds me like a child and caresses me like I'm a woman. A comforting sense of security envelopes me in warmth and I drift off to sleep without worry of nightmares.

Grigor is already up when I waken from a deep, refreshing sleep. Gesturing to my morning wood he offers *I can take care of that for you*, but I just laugh and tell him *it'll fix itself with a piss*.

When I return to my bedroom he hands me a steaming mug of black coffee. He's still naked so I don't bother to dress either. I know Grigor's feeling for me is more than loyalty and friendship but, he never pushes. On the many occasions we've had sex I always initiated it. I am his Alpha.

The two of us get back into bed to savor our hot drinks sitting propped up by pillows. He begins a serious conversation but there's no hint of criticism in his questions and comments. I find myself opening up to my friend and once I start the words keep coming.

"The first time I had sex I was fourteen. That was older than either of my brothers but I had to wait for my balls to drop. You were there, the whole pack witnessed the ritual. A coming-of-age for young wolves when one of our Omegas went into heat.

What a mind-blowing experience that was! Way more, much much more, than I ever imagined it would be. I was hooked and wanted to fuck non-stop every hour of every day. Sex was all I could think about."

Grigor replies: "We still have initiations but infrequently. Our population growth has slowed meaning we don't have the same number of young people to celebrate the milestone. I remember your rite-of-passage very well. I was still a teenager and allowed to participate too. Those Omegas... fuckin' hot, huh?"

"And for a couple of years life revolved around sex and *nagy cicik [big tits]*—"

Grigor interrupts with the happy declaration: "It still does!"

I laugh at his enthusiasm. "Remember how it was, after a wild run with the pack, when the she-wolves were always willing to be claimed for a rut. And when the Omegas went into heat, fuck yeah that was... hmmm," I smile in memory of those simple days of unrestrained, guilt-free pleasure.

"It changed for you when you got involved with Beáta," Grigor quietly states.

I nod in agreement, my mind going back to the time when I noticed Beata as a female sexual being and not just a girl from school.

"She was different because she was human. She didn't have heats so it wasn't easy to get her thighs apart. I had to woo and seduce her and when I did it was such an achievement... it really made me feel like a man. She was my first – and only – virgin lover. I fell head over heels in love with her."

The recollection is as bright and beautiful as it was seven or eight years earlier. Beáta's skin was so soft, her mouth eager, her eyes apprehensive but still she entrusted herself to me. That trust. The power she gave me with her faith, her belief in me.

We'd had so many necking sessions, my hands always roving but never too insistent, and my balls aching by time we kissed goodnight. Until that first time. It wasn't even at night, we weren't finishing up a date.

No, it was in the afternoon when Beáta called inviting me to come over to her place.

When I got there no one else was at home and she led me to her bedroom. I remember her saying *my parents took my sister to visit with my cousins her age and they'll be gone for hours.* Those hours passed so fast!

Beáta was eager to experience sex and I was desperate to get inside her. Our first time was full of tender feelings, of care and concern and love. After that day we made love every chance we got over the next six or seven months.

"You had the true *Girlfriend Experience* and fell in love."

I feel my eyelids prickle and squint until the waterworks fade. "That memory belongs in the past. I don't want to speak of it anymore."

"Okay Alpha, that subject is closed. Besides, it's way more important for me to know: *when's the last time you shifted?*"

I shrug off the question but he persists. "Antal, you reek of frustrated wolf. It's a strong, sour stink. It's your wolf's final, desperate ploy for attention, to be freed."

"Shifters aren't welcome here in America." I speak coldly, hoping to deter him, but I should have known better. Grigor's only just arrived in the country but he's come armed with introductions and contacts.

I try to explain why I avoid the shifter community but my excuses don't ring true. I realize I've been hiding my wolf from shame which is misplaced and wrong because my wolf never committed a crime. That's all on my human self.

The warped perversion of torture followed by vicious and violent fucking... that's not the way of the wolf. A predator, sure, but with a purpose. Not just for sick twisted pleasure.

Grigor senses my embarrassed reluctance and announces we'll begin with just the two of us. We've shifted countless times in the past and can easily do so again.

"Yeah okay, I can do that," I agree.

"Great, let's go," he says standing and dragging me from my bed.

"What, now? Why? What's the rush?" I backpedal, throwing up excuses.

"The rush is my wolf is crying for the pain your wolf is in this very minute and mine's demanding we fix it right now."

I huff, but he ignores my complaint. Soon we're in the car with me driving while he follows an app on his phone and directs me to one of the State forests. I've never been here before and am awed by the size of the trees and the large swath of land the government has preserved.

We park and head out on the trail only to veer off when we find a suitable spot to shed our clothes and transform. I hesitate, anxious and overly cautious because it's been years, but Grigor's steady encouragement compels me. He coaxes my wolf to the surface of consciousness.

The moment my wolf emerges my senses are awakened to vivid colors, fragrant scents, and soothing sounds. The undergrowth is viridescent, the flowers are perfumed, and in the distance I hear the clatter of water pouring down onto rocks.

I stretch every muscle in every limb and howl with the pleasure of it all. I savor the freedom and freshness of this dense forest of old growth trees. I snap my jaw with joy.

Bounding deeper into the woods I hear Grigor close behind me, following where I lead. My tongue flies out the side of my mouth and a breeze ripples through the hair along my neck and back. Entering a small clearing I throw myself down to wriggle on the mossy ground. My paws are pedaling in the air and I swear Grigor is laughing at me.

"Olyan jóképű vagy farkas [You are so handsome, wolf]" he teases.

I resist his attempts to drive me back towards the parking lot. I'm experiencing true freedom and am no where near ready for this to end.

But after a couple of hours I start to flag and the pads of my paws are sore from stepping on sticks, stones, and thorns. I'm drooling heavily and searching for refreshment when we locate a rushing brook. The air is full of negative ions that invigorate me and I dip my head to drink deep. Nature provides everything a wolf needs.

A stifled scream alerts us to several humans in hiking gear. A wicked thought tempts me to snarl and chase them away, but Grigor nudges me to turn around and escape back into the bracken. He's always made it his duty to guard me from danger even when - maybe *especially* when - it comes from my own impulses.

We retrieve our clothes and shift back to dress. I can't find the words to express the strength of my feelings and just before we get to my car I burst into tears. It's a humiliating release of emotion but I just can't stop it.

Grigor helps me into the passenger seat and I sit there in silence, my head bowed in shame. Grigor reaches over to clasp the back of my neck and gently squeeze. The tears stream down my face and I'm trembling with relief all while struggling to regain control of myself.

He understands. More than I do. His presence nourishes me, feeding my soul. He's directing me back onto the right path for a shifter, and he's at my side for every step of this journey. His friendship is invaluable.

Our days together stretch into weeks, months, and eventually a couple of years pass by. I was on my own, a loner, for so long but my Beta's company invigorates me. We speak Hungarian, he cooks us traditional food, and we regularly shift together. He's brought me back to life.

Mentally I'm still steeped in debauchery so I continue to accept those contracted kills involving punishment and retribution. I can unleash the devil in me then although Grigor's devoted guardianship helps me keep him under control the rest of the time.

Grigor attracts submissive women who are drawn to the manliness of his size. He brings them home promising he will tempt them into a *ménage à trois*. They're curious but unwilling to commit. Until they meet me and then my good looks and practiced smile have them readily consenting to bed both of us. They never notice that my smile doesn't reach my eyes.

In these scenarios I often pretend I've found another Bridgette to play with. She was the embodiment of the sheer pleasure of unfettered sex. A union rather than a conquering. My memory of that happy encounter has kept me anchored many times over the years when I've worried over the kind of man I've become.

I made it clear to Grigor I will only participate if the women look nothing like Beáta. I don't want to risk unleashing my beast.

Grigor is such a big man we can only comfortably manage the bed if he lies on the bottom with the girl riding him in *reverse cowgirl style* so I can fuck her face. If they're willing Grigor will pull the girl down to his chest so I can take their ass. That's my preference.

It was a surprise to both of us to discover how few of these women are anal virgins. I never realized human women enjoyed that type of intercourse. From their cries of pleasure it seems they revel in the sensation of *being stuffed so full* by double penetration. I know for she-wolves it's the dominance of the act that appeals.

We've loosely connected with a local community for pack runs but they keep their Omegas hidden from us. The protective instincts an Alpha feels towards his Omega, particularly when she's in heat, make that understandable.

Now that I'm shifting again I find myself yearning for an Omega to claim as my own. I miss the wanton headiness of the lustful romps I knew as a youth. There's nothing like having a girl begging and whining with need to make a boy feel like a man. To make a wolf know he's an Alpha.

Sadly, I've never knotted a female. There's so little chance of finding an unattached Omega that I gave up on finding my fated mate a long time ago.

Grigor and I also have adventures with high-class call girls we hire to entertain us in luxury suites. It's still mostly normal sex, group sex, but it's so much easier when you're paying for it. You can just tell them what you want done instead of trying to earn consent.

When I feel the compulsion to hurt a Beáta-type I go out alone, but am confident Grigor is always somewhere nearby, watching my back.

This zest for life that I have now makes me interested in growing my illegal import/export business. The dull ennui I'd fallen into no longer holds me back. I'm driven to build my empire and make a name for myself as more than a contracted killer and sadistic torturer.

With Grigor's help I invest more time and effort into weapons procurements with my Eastern European partners. We acquire a reputation for providing a quality product with secure, expedited shipping. Eventually I reunite with organizations that do business with my family back in Hungary. Our working relationships are profitable, I respect the leaders, and I'm thriving. It's a turn of the wheel, what the gypsies of my youth call *Rota Fortunae*, bringing me back closer to my beginning.

I've scheduled a secret meeting with Sandor Koczinyi and Janos Erdős, two powerful Alphas who worked closely with my father, and Grigor is driving me to the location now. It's taking place in the southern part of the state, at a private club where we know the owner. These clan leaders are only staying the one day and will fly right out again.

This meeting is hush-hush so we can finalize the new route for our merchandise. The Alphas tell me that back in Hungary a rival gang comprised of humans, the Fehers, dogs their every step. These *baszós [fuckers]* are determinedly trying to encroach on shifter territory.

Grigor and I have taken our time getting here. He's never been in this part of California so we detoured to see some of the popular sights. Now we're following the GPS on his phone and have left the lights of the downtown core to head into an industrial area.

"What's this place called again?"

"*The Gentlemen's Club*," I reply with a smirk.

"Seriously? It's a men's club that they actually called *The Gentlemen's Club*? Not very original."

"Maybe it makes more sense in English, I don't know. The owner, a Hungarian called Milán, has sly-smarts but he's not very clever. He fawns over guests and then bullies his staff to make him feel like a man again."

"He's human?"

"Yeah, but he knows all about shifters. He grew up in the same neighborhood where Beáta lived, but he moved to California many years ago."

The AI's female voice leads us to finish up on a street of storefront offices with warehouses attached at the back. *The Gentlemen's Club* stands out from its utilitarian-looking neighbors with newly painted shutters and window trim, and fragrant flowering bushes growing green against the red brick of the building.

"Everything's closed and it's Saturday night," exclaims Grigor in surprise. "They can't do much business here in this location."

"This Milán told me the place is busy from noon until early evening on weekdays. The workers come for a drink at lunch time and often spend the rest of the afternoon in the bar. Another wave comes in when all the businesses close. They don't stay open late at night.

Of course that didn't stop him trying to charge big bucks to shut down this place for our meeting. Trouble is, he forgot he'd originally said *no* because they were planning to close tonight anyhow. Something about a festival or a fair all his workers want to attend."

Grigor just shakes his head at the owner's foolish greed. He follows behind his Alpha until Antal opens the door and is greeted

89

enthusiastically. Grigor returns to wait with the car for what he's sure will be a long, uneventful night.

* * *

What happens next? Read on for the first two chapters of Lockdown + 3 Alphas = Heat

"Lockdown + 3 Alphas = Heat"
Chapter 1

Fuck. My. Life.

Tonight's the biggest party of the DECADE and I can't go. Why? Because three Alpha-holes have booked this crummy private club for the evening and I have to stay and serve them. Wearing a stupid costume that doesn't even fit right.

Why? Because the real hostesses get to go to the County Decennial Celebration taking place in Vista Valley so oh hey, guess who is suddenly good enough to do a servers job?

This is such bullshit. I'll be too old to really enjoy myself by time the next Decennial party rolls around. I'll be like.. thirty.

Both Mandy and Marcie practically laughed themselves sick at me being stuck behind. They're almost mirror images of each other: tall, one golden-blonde the other strawberry-blonde, natural C cups, legs that go on forever, but that old saying about beauty only being skin-deep might have been written for them. They're nasty, spiteful, hateful girls who like to push me around.

Then there's me, Lake, although no one actually calls me by my name. I'm skinny, have white-blonde hair, barely an A cup bra size, and scrawny legs. I look like a cross between a starving ghost and a gawky, consumptive child. Mandy calls me Puddle and the nickname has stuck. I guess I should be thankful no one's thought of Mud Puddle.

I do all the drudge work at this A-list Gentlemens Club called, with great originality, the A-list Gentlemens Club. I guess having the same slogan and business name saves a lot on advertising. I think it's stupid but, to be fair, today everything feels stupid. Especially me.

I called it a crummy club but truth is it's really nice. A red-brick building with white window sills and shutters, and lots of green ivy, that turns pretty shades of red in the Fall, climbing the walls. It looks good, but I'm not a fan of the bees it attracts.

The floors are all ceramic tile or marble, and there are lots of thick Persian rugs and runners. Plenty of pictures on the walls with heavy-looking ornate frames in gold. They're all of naked women but since they're oil paintings instead of photos I guess that makes them art instead of porn.

It's a man's club – supposedly for gentlemen – so the big, heavy furniture is made of dark wood and leather in burgundy and forest green. It smells good with the lingering smoke from expensive cigars and high-priced aftershave and cologne.

I'm strictly back-of-house meaning washing dishes then bussing dishes so I can wash some more. The kitchen is crap. Well, I guess it's good for the chef, he's got all the fancy chrome stuff, but the floors here are linoleum, all cracked so you know that means they're really old and hard to clean, and the counters are formica. I didn't know the names of these things until I heard the staff complaining that we're probably all inhaling asbestos.

All the money gets spent on the members areas and nothing on improving the working conditions back here. These back rooms also have florescent lighting which has an unpleasant hum. No wonder I'm so pale, always stuck in the far corner of the kitchen.

I'm twenty years old but I look about fourteen because I'm a runt. I get picked on and bullied, taken for granted and used. Although I'm a wolf-shifter I spent my childhood as a human having been a rescued foundling infant. Raised in an orphanage I was able to go to school where I discovered an affinity with numbers and a love of reading: quiet non-physical activities.

It also meant I was taught nothing about my wolf nature, a side of me I didn't even know existed until at age sixteen, late from undernourishment, I hit puberty. Like a truck slamming full-speed into a brick wall. Adolescent angst pales compared to adolescent wolf angst.

Raging hormones turned me from an unloved and miserable wimp into a vicious temperamental fighter. The first time I shifted was involuntary and I thought I'd been bitten by a werewolf unawares. As if that could happen, wolf bites hurt plenty!

I got kicked out of the home and had to live off the streets – the same fate my own kind had abandoned me to all those years before: to starve in the street like a mutt. That's where I met some other shifters, not all of them wolves, and learned a little about who and what I was.

But I was leery of strangers, afraid of everyone, or at least unable to trust anyone. Fear turned me into a scrapper but my too-small size meant I lost most fights.

Shifting was a difficult and painful process at first but I practiced and practiced and eventually got it down pat. Unfortunately city streets are no place for a wolf. Since cis-humans attack what frightens them the safest places I could find were in derelict, sparsely populated areas. That's how I found the alleyway behind The Gentlemens Club and eventually wormed my way inside as a menial worker.

No one there knows I can shift, but when the mean hostesses bully me sometimes it's really hard to keep my wolf nature in check. But, for overall survival, I need to keep that truth hidden by keeping my head down.

I'm certainly the most unthreatening-looking person ever! Inadequate feeding has left me with zero resistance so I catch every germ around and am usually sniffling or sneezing. When my nose isn't red I have no color at all.

Well, okay I do have the most amazing eyes. When I look in the mirror I even shock myself. It was a teacher, way back when, who first called them aquamarine and she taught me how to spell the word. It's the only exotic-sounding thing about me.

Okay, enough of the pity-party, right? I'd rather be angry than mopey. And I have good reason, too. I mean, they NEVER, EVER let me serve in the Club, especially when there are visiting VIPs, but yeah when everybody else wants to go to the big party well then it's a different story. Suddenly it's *oh sure, Puddle can take care of the VIPs.*

I was already cranky and this has really pissed me off. Especially since these guests are wolves, too. I've had very little interaction with fellow shifters and I've always avoided Alphas: aggressive, domineering, intimidating males. Ugh!

Milán, the Club Manager who might even be the owner because that's a bit of a mystery, must not care too much about these Alpha-holes to stick them with me, though. Of course I think they're pond-scum to insist on a private function in the Club tonight of all nights. Maybe Milán has just said *sorry, but she's the best I can do, everyone else has booked off.*

I won't be talking to the Alpha-holes because they don't speak English and I don't speak anything else. I guess we'll be playing charades! Actually it won't be too bad because they didn't show up here until eleven, after dinner anyways, so I just have to serve drinks and some snack food. They each arrived separately and with an interval between.

All very hush-hush. They want privacy so hopefully they'll be happy if I bring out a selection of bottles and let them serve themselves.

That would be best for me because my crankiness isn't just at missing out on the party of the decade, no, it's also hormonal. I'm in pre-heat. I should be okay for at least one more day, I'm not lubricating yet, but even if these men are Alpha-holes they're still Alphas and that scares me. If my scent turns really sweet I'm afraid I'll trigger them to rut. One coming after me will be bad enough but three? They'll fight each other and tear me apart in the process.

I'm calling them #1, #2, and #3 but of course they do have names. First is Sandor and I call him #1 because he's the oldest. Second – #2 – is Janos the chatty one, and #3 is called Antal-the-Gorgeous.

Despite everything I have to admit these are three hunky men who look like they stepped off the pages of GQ magazine. The Eastern European edition. Especially Antal. He truly looks like a male model if the ad is for what the well-dressed hired killer is wearing this season. Including tattoos on the back of his hands, and probably everywhere else, too.

And not those cheap jail tattoos of L-O-V-E and H-A-T-E across his knuckles, oh no, these are a swirling pattern of skulls and roses and trailing ivy and twisting snakes. My eyes want to follow them up his arms.

They're all dressed in expensive well-tailored suits that can't disguise their muscular physiques under what looks like very pricey cloth. Their weapons are well-hidden, though. Nobody has a paunch, and neatly trimmed beards hide any double-chins. The tidy barbering extends to hair cut stylishly short.

Oh great, Milán, speaking in their own language, has just introduced me and now they're all having a laugh. The Alpha-holes glance my way with amusement and I'm not impressed. I don't care that their smiles show off healthy white teeth and handsome faces that crinkle round the eyes, eyes that seem to have a very penetrating focus.

I'm sure I've got a sullen, sulky expression but that just seems to entertain them. Milán turns to me saying they think my name is a joke and they're going to call me *Tó* which is Lake in Hungarian, but only because *Tócsa,* meaning Puddle, is too long.

Bunch of freakin' comedians.

So they're Hungarian. That's where the gypsies come from, right? I thought that ethnic group were short-statured with dark hair and dark complexions – well, except for the vampires, that is – but these men are sandy or fair-haired and tall and big. Of course since I have to take a deep breath to measure five feet high everyone looks big and tall to me.

A fourth man, Kartal, came in with them and he's somebody's Beta but I didn't pay much attention so I don't know whose. He speaks English and can translate but he didn't stay long. Apparently Kartal will be waiting outside with the vehicles and drivers. The three men want complete privacy to transact some business they're setting up here in America.

I'm sure that even if I understood their language I wouldn't count, I'm used to being overlooked. Even dressed as slutty as I am right now. It's ridiculous to put me into the same gear that the hostesses wear. The uniform consists of a strapless black top and black french-cut panties with a red heart sewn over the pubic mound.

Mandy and Marcie's boobs strain to escape their tube tops while I can barely keep mine up. I don't fill out the panties very well either. Neither do I have an interesting navel piercing nor a tramp stamp tattoo. I don't even have a suntan.

I do have a nice ass if you like such tight little buns that can be held in one hand but that's hardly the fashion these days. At least when I wobble about in these skyscraper high-heels there's nothing jiggling. Sad to say that's not because I'm taut and toned but because I have nothing to jiggle.

Damn, now I'm sounding whiny and miserable again. It's another symptom of being pre-heat.

After a flurry of conversation Milán leaves. He's on his way to join the party in Vista Valley, the next town over. I'm sure it will be in full swing by time he arrives. I hope he eats a bad hotdog and burps for the rest of the night making everyone pull away from his bad breath.

So now I'm here alone with my three VIPs who seem quite content to ignore me and be ignored right back. Milán told me what booze to fetch and it takes me a couple of trips to bring it all out. Scotch whiskey, American bourbon, Portuguese brandy, tumblers and snifters.

Once the drinks are taken care of I hover uncertainly not knowing what I should be doing but #3 slaps me on the butt and makes a shooing gesture. I want to give him a dirty look but after glancing into his dark shark eyes, such a dramatic contrast with is light-brown hair, I'm glad to escape while I can. Even as my body gives a little shudder of pleasurable fear. Why is it always the most handsome one who is the meanest prick? Is there a connection between beauty and a nasty nature? Maybe. That would certainly explain why Mandy and Marcie behave the way they do.

Anyhow, I scuttle away since my plan is to hide out in the kitchen, in my little nook, and try to get some sleep. I'm sure the men will make sufficient noise to wake me if they want anything – don't men always?

"Lockdown + 3 Alphas = Heat"
Chapter 2

So much for grabbing a nap. We've got law enforcement driving heavy vehicles up and down the street broadcasting that everyone has to stay indoors. We're in lockdown. There's a manhunt on in the area for an escaped killer convict.

"Remain inside for your safety. Do not open windows or doors. Do not leave the premises. There's an armed and dangerous man outside. Armed police and tactical units are patrolling."

No one can enter or leave any of the properties. Anyone already on the street is being detained and questioned. Anyone breaking the rules could be shot! What if this crazed killer has already breached some place and is holding somebody hostage?

Now they're banging on the doors yelling at us to stay inside. Of course my Alpha-holes don't understand a word of it and haven't got a clue what's going on. They don't like the official-sounding announcement or the yelling. Naturally they want to go outside to see what's happening and I'm standing in front of the door shaking my head and saying *No! No! No!* Like they're going to pay the slightest bit of attention to me.

Just as they're getting ready to get rough – experience has taught me to sense when the blows are coming – we all hear a loud rapid knocking coming from the kitchen door. A muffled voice is calling so the four of us head that way. I hate to let the Alpha-holes anywhere near my hidey-hole but it can't be helped.

The rat-a-tat is loud and frenzied and the voice is becoming clearer. It's Kartal, the Beta, and he's calling out:

"Miss Lake! Miss Lake! Get my Alpha, Miss Lake! It's urgent!"

"Kartal? They're all here, I don't know which one is yours."

He doesn't bother to answer me and instead launches into their language and soon all of them are yelling at each other and back-and-forth through the door. Then Kartal switches to English explaining, to a cop I guess, what he's doing.

"Miss Lake he's taking me away! Make sure they stay inside! They MUST stay inside! I told them animals are being shot so no shifting to escape."

After a brief scuffling noise, probably Kartal being dragged up the steps to the alley, we don't hear anything more from outside. A couple of vehicle doors slam – maybe that's the police taking Kartal away?

The Alpha-holes are furious and I don't need to speak Hungarian to figure that out. There's only a small window in the kitchen which looks out onto the cement staircase since we're in the basement. The three men hurry back to look out the windows in the main room but at the A-list Gentlemens Club they're all shuttered on the outside.

Great, now we're all stuck here, and what if it's for longer than just one night? The men turn on one of the big screen TVs but nothing happens except an error message saying no signal.

I stay in the kitchen and switch on the little portable radio but there's no news broadcast. Every station is playing music because it is Saturday night, after all. I start hunting for something with a strong odor to mask my sweetening scent. I can't find any garlic but the organics bin holds the peelings from an onion. I rub it over my hands and the red heart crotch of my uniform panties and mentally cross my fingers.

I can hear the Alpha-holes from here as they bitch and complain. At least that's what I'm assuming, it all sounds very angry and destructive. I guess I need to go see if they want anything but that's going to be tricky when I can't understand a word they say.

The irony of this lockdown is that I know all three of these Alpha-holes are murderers themselves. Probably even more dangerous than the escapee. I'm trapped inside with killers, and I'm absolutely certain these guys are armed.

Also by Lori Laidlaw

Alpha + Omega Wolf-Shifters
Dominant + Violent + Hot = An Alpha Male

Standalone
Lockdown + 3 Alphas = Heat: An Omega's Thrilling Dark Romantic
Adventure
Girlie: Undeniable Attraction Enemies to Lovers Steamy Standalone
Cruel Obligation
Jane's Special Adventure
Captive's Deception
Finn and Marbeth
"Princess Weds Killer" = Fake News

Watch for more at https://lori-laidlaw-novelist-
bvwonn.mailerpage.io/.

About the Author

Lori says:

I'm a bit shy... but I love reading and writing in the Adult Romance genre with all its sub-categories.

I fall in love with my characters whose moods range from playful to dangerous and everything in between!

My stories are multiple POV expressing mature themes and passionate encounters with enough steam to stimulate your imagination.

It's all about the love.

Email: AuthorLoriLaidlaw@gmail.com

Website: https://lori-laidlaw-novelist-bvwonn.mailerpage.io/

Facebook: https://www.facebook.com/people/Author-Lori-Laidlaw/61555470454210/

Goodreads: https://www.goodreads.com/author/show/29566696.Lori_Laidlaw

Read more at https://lori-laidlaw-novelist-bvwonn.mailerpage.io/.